# CANE FIRES

# CANE FIRES

KAUI PHILPOTTS

*Cane Fires*

Published by Mango Tree Publishing



ISBN: 978-1-7327867-0-7

Library of Congress Control Number: 2018902035

Cover Artist: Nuno Moreira

Book Designer: Sarah Katreen Hoggatt

10 9 8 7 6 5 4 3 2 1

*Cane Fires* is a work of fiction. The story, characters, places, and incidents are imaginary creations of the author or are used fictitiously. Any resemblance between these fictional characters and actual persons, living or dead, or events or locales, is purely coincidental.

# CONTENTS

# DOLORES

LENA KAMAKA'S BIG MAROON DESOTO SAT in the front yard under a shower tree. Blossoms the color of lemons covered the ground, one or two having landed on the car's hood. Lena's presence meant one thing: They were getting a new maid.

Lily and her brother, Hank, spent the morning playing epic war survival games in the bushes near a row of dilapidated garages a block away. Stealing plots from Saturday movie matinees and pretending to be war refugees were their favorite pastimes. All summer long, sheets, pillows, and kitchen items went missing from the house. Their mother, Clare, was so uninterested in housekeeping she rarely missed the items.

Hank was ten, two years younger than Lily. Lately she'd started to tire of their play, making excuses to stay in her room, attempting to make her bone-straight hair look more like that of her favorite movie stars. Lily also began to notice boys, and Hank's silliness sometimes annoyed her.

The two had been engrossed in play all morning. But when they spotted Lena Kamaka's DeSoto, they hoped they hadn't missed the spectacle of the detention-home matron lowering herself to her usual spot on their living room *punee*. She was a giantess. So big, in fact, it was difficult for her to make it up the flight of stairs to their front door. Lily and Hank hid and watched as she placed her ample bottom smack in the center of the creaky punee their mother had created from an old iron bed. With help from the young Japanese girls attending Mrs. Kimura's sewing classes, Clare had covered the daybed with tropical-printed fabric.

The punee usually let out a painful wail as it dipped perilously close to the floor in an attempt to support Lena Kamaka. But today the formidable woman was already safely installed in her spot, speaking quietly to their mother. Clare nodded and the two laughed, but the children couldn't make out what Lena was saying. Bored after a few minutes of straining to hear, they gave up and crept out through the kitchen door and headed next door to see what kind of trouble they could get into.

From the neighbor's window, Lily and Hank saw the maroon station wagon pulling out into the street, and at the same time the whistle from the sugar mill blasted loud and clear. It was five o'clock and soon time to head home.

THE NEXT DAY, LENA KAMAKA WAS back again, this time with a small, dark-skinned girl of about sixteen. She wore a pair of men's Levi's rolled to her knees. On top was an oversized man's *kabe* silk shirt with a large, ferocious-looking Asian tiger crawling across her back. Clare showed the girl down a dimly lit hallway off the kitchen, past the linen closet to two small rooms that would be hers.

The girl began unpacking a small suitcase and putting her clothes in drawers. Lily and Hank, bursting with curiosity, watched through a crack in the open door. She didn't have much to unpack—a small stack of T-shirts, a couple of cotton dresses, and one pair of shoes.

"You can come in if you want to!" came the cheerful, throaty voice from inside. The girl stared back at them through the opening in the door. The maid's room was off limits, which was precisely why it held endless fascination. *Imagine a place in our house we've never explored*, they thought. "Off limits!" was an automatic challenge.

"Come on in," the girl said again, holding the door wide open. Sheepishly, they moved into the forbidden territory.

In one corner of the bedroom, a single iron bed painted white and covered in pale pink chenille was pushed against the wall. Clare had ordered it from the Sears catalogue in an attempt to freshen the room. Against the other wall was a cream-colored vanity and, above it, an oval mirror etched with tiny pink and green pastel flowers. They were castoffs, Lily noticed, but taken together as a whole, they looked fresh, sweet, and feminine. Lily suspected it might have been the first room of the girl's own by the careful way she placed her hairbrush and toilet articles on the vanity.

"I'm Dolores. So what are your names?" she said, smiling from ear to ear with the biggest mouthful of teeth they'd ever seen. Lily and Hank liked Dolores immediately. Her brown skin was smooth, and her hair, cut to her shoulders, was black with a distinctive red tint. She had obviously made an attempt to keep her hair in check with pin curls at night but had clearly failed. For them, the idea of Dolores was full of mischief and the promise of fun. They recognized a kindred spirit immediately.

IN THE WEEKS THAT FOLLOWED, LILY and Hank followed Dolores everywhere. They hung out with her after lunch when she took starched, sprinkled clothes rolled in plastic out of the refrigerator and began ironing on the back porch, the radio blasting the ballads of Perry Como and Rosemary Clooney.

The two learned to say "shi-it!" and Dolores let them listen to the radio soap operas their mother never allowed, *Stella Dallas* and *One Life to Live*. This led to heated discussions about the infidelities and bad behaviors the characters acted out on a daily basis.

On Saturdays, their father, Buddy, gave Dolores two dollars to take the kids to a movie. Buddy spent Saturdays hunting or fishing with his friends. Sometimes the friends were from the plantation office, but more often his friends lived in the Japanese camps nearby. They all loved talking politics and drinking beer when they got home with their birds or fish. The drinking made Buddy's handsome, tanned face glow beet red.

Clare never joined in and neither did the other wives. She'd always had help with the children. No one ever said it out loud, but everyone knew she really couldn't cope with children any more than she could do housework. They were too noisy, messy, and unruly, and she lacked patience. "High-strung" was how she was described.

"Indians!" Clare's older sister Emma shouted unkindly to Lily and Hank when they visited their grandmother. "Here come the Donahue Indians!" Clare stuck her nose in the air and managed to ignore her.

But she was still young, barely thirty. She had been nineteen, and Buddy a decade older, when he brought her from Wailuku to live on the plantation. For his young bride, it might as well have been an entire continent away. She was lost in plantation life with its subtle rules and not-so-subtle racial and class distinctions. Being *hapa haole,* or half white, probably didn't help matters either. Very few Hawaiians found their way onto plantations, preferring to work in civil service or independently on the land or sea.

It was easy to see what had attracted Buddy. Clare had a voluptuousness that was surprising on her tiny frame. Her hair was dark and unruly, bordering on wild bushiness. But it was her eyes that struck everyone bold enough to look directly into them. They were large and brown with a vaguely faraway quality. Her dreaminess, punctuated every now and then by a mercurial, spicy temperament, made the other plantation wives, many from the Midwest, uncomfortable. She was too different and unpredictable. There was no place for Clare in the neighborhood reserved for plantation upper management.

Clare tried making friends with Susie Foster next door. Susie was always very nice, bringing over freshly baked banana bread and cookies on the days she baked. But Clare was never invited to Susie's luncheons with the women from her tennis or book groups.

Clare had just two friends. One was Sara Cole, who lived down the street and was married to a German engineer. She, too, was Hawaiian, but darker skinned and more ample than Clare, and on her chin was a large black mole with two long hairs curving downward. Sara was at least fifteen years older and a comfort to Clare, with her local island ways. But Sara was often busy with her own life.

Clare's other friend was Aggie Mendez. Aggie had been a teenager when she came to live with the Donahues. She had still been in high school then and had cooked, cleaned, and ironed in exchange for the small rooms that were now inhabited by Dolores.

From the day she moved in, the two had been friends. They'd laughed and gossiped while making dinner together before Buddy came home. Aggie had liked to bake Portuguese bread that Clare and the children devoured, still warm, with thick slabs of fresh butter. On the weekends, they packed bologna sandwiches and a thermos of Kool-Aid and drove to the beach near Kuau where the children swam. Clare and Aggie sat in the sand, caught up in conversation.

But Aggie graduated from high school and moved to Honolulu to study stenography, leaving Clare alone again. Shortly after, Lena Kamaka began showing up with other young girls who would live with them and help around the house. These girls were different. They usually were in trouble, or had had trouble brought upon them. They lived in the county detention facility in Wailuku. You took your chances with these girls, and some of them had lasted only a couple of weeks before Lena Kamaka was back to collect them. Lily and Hank were always on their best behavior until they figured the girls out. Who knew what they were capable of doing, or what they already had done to land in such a frightening place?

ON DOLORES'S FIRST SATURDAY WITH THE Donahues, Lily and Hank walked with her from their house in Haole Camp, with its big shady trees and rolling lawns, through the Portuguese camp, with its pristine sidewalks scrubbed with Clorox and bread ovens peeking from the backyards. There were always pungent sausage and cabbage smells wafting out the screen doors. The aromas of soups full of cinnamon and cloves and freshly baked breads assaulted them again that day.

Movies at the theater—a large, wooden, featureless structure with a small, round box office in front—was hands down their favorite thing to do on weekend afternoons.

Dolores's first visit to the theater created quite a stir. Dressed in her signature skintight jeans and a tight red-and-white-striped T-shirt, she cut quite a swath past the lines of Portuguese and Puerto Rican boys hanging out near the concession stand. They had just rubbed out their illegal cigarettes on the concrete floor with their slippers and were about to head to their usual seats down front near the screen.

Lily and Hank bought *mochi* crunch, *li hing mui* seeds, and packs of Violet candy and headed to their usual seats in front of the loge section where the old haole ladies always sat at the popular movies—the ones starring Clark Cable and Rita Hayworth, and, of course, there were the Judy Garland musicals.

On that day, they were well past the Hopalong Cassidy serial and into the main feature before they realized Dolores was no longer sitting with them. She'd found one of the Nobriga boys and was sitting down front. This part of the theater was off limits to them. It was understood that this was where the bad boys sat—the ones who smoked, whistled from passing cars, and slouched around outside the gym wearing ducktail hairdos and pegged pants.

But Dolores was clearly having a very good time, and Lily and Hank soon forgot about her and lost themselves in Fred Astaire's dancing. They thought Dolores was wonderful, the way she laughed at everything they said and talked to them as if they were as grown up and worldly as she.

THE THEATER AND NEARBY GYM WERE hangouts for all the young boys in Paia. The town began along the ocean, at what everyone referred to as Lower Paia. It wasn't much more than a strip of mom-and-pop stores run by Japanese and Chinese who left the plantation when their contracts were up and were now involved in private enterprises.

There was Harada's gas station, a mercantile store, Molina's Bar, and Hew Store that served fresh, crinkled saimin noodles and rich, salty, homemade broth. On rainy days, Clare took a large pot from the kitchen and drove to the restaurant to have it filled with hot saimin to take home for lunch.

Baldwin Avenue continued up toward Haleakala Crater, past cane fields and a *punawai*, or reservoir, to the mill, the medical dispensary, the company store, and, finally, the workers' houses.

Every weekday was regulated by a blast of the horn from the mill. It told workers when to get up, when to have lunch, and when their father was finished work in the plantation office. Even as an old woman, Lily would remember the blast in the middle of the day, the sun high and bright in the sky, and the breeze blowing through the avocado tree near the back door. It was how they lived their lives and marked their days.

THE STICKY, HOT SUMMER DAYS DRONED on. Clare and Dolores packed up lunches and took the kids to the beach, as she and Aggie had done. Dolores loved these outings. Lily and Hank played in the tide pools, while she tanned herself on the sand nearby, lying on a brilliant pink beach towel with mermaids and shells printed all over it.

"Bet you nevah seen green sand," Dolores said as Lily plopped down beside her. "I seen beaches as green as anything. Just like jewels."

"You lie!" she squealed to Dolores. "There's no such thing!" Hank had dropped down near Lily and was kicking sand at her to get her attention.

"Like jewels, huh?" Lily said, squinting in disbelief. How could she be so worldly? How could she know about so many things?

The three of them looked for *puka* shells and sometimes found larger shells still filled with sea animals. They buried those in the flower bed outside the kitchen door and let the ants clean them out. Then, in the afternoon, Dolores helped them string the shells into necklaces before she was called to help prepare dinner.

At night, they had to be pried from Dolores's little room to go to bed. Clare ignored her rule about not going into the maid's room because it gave her more time alone with Buddy, and they all seemed to be having so much fun.

It was around this time when Lily realized Dolores had been sneaking out of her room at night.

"You know dat Wally Perreira?" Dolores said one day when she and Lily were paging through *True Confessions* magazines looking for the juicy parts.

"Yeah," Lily answered. She was aware he spent a lot of time in the detention home, too. Lily hadn't the slightest idea what Wally had done to put himself there, but whatever he'd done, it sure wasn't good.

"I think he's killer sexy. Whaddaya think?" she said, raising her eyebrows in a knowing way and smiling from ear to ear with those big teeth. Lily got a queasy feeling in her stomach. She wasn't totally clueless about the facts of life; her mother had begun leaving pamphlets around with diagrams of fallopian tubes, but she hadn't yet put all the little bits of information together to make a whole picture.

"Oh, yeah," Lily answered, pretending to know more than she did, but she was starting to feel uncomfortable. Still, being taken into the confidence of this dangerously joyful, noisy girl seemed much more important than her discomfort.

"I see him all the time, you know."

"You don't! When?"

"At night. After everyone asleep. I climb out da window. Everyone's on da other end of the house anyways."

"Dolores! They're going to catch you and send you back to the detention home. You shouldn't do that!"

Lily suddenly felt desperate. Maids had never been this much fun. They always treated you like a kid and then hid themselves away in their room. They didn't hang out on beaches with green jewels and string puka shells or talk to you as if you were as grown up and sophisticated as they were.

"They won't know if you no tell," she whispered, coyly fingering one of the pink curlers in her hair.

*Tell them! I'd never do such a thing*, thought Lily. And ruin the most freedom she'd ever had?

AT THE END OF AUGUST, LILY'S parents received an invitation to a party at the plantation manager's home. It was obviously a big deal because Clare spent a long time talking to Sara Cole on the phone about what to wear and who was going to be there. She even went down to the plantation store and bought a new dress. It was strapless, with a full skirt made of black lace over something flesh-colored that made her look very sultry, even dangerous. Like Hedy Lamarr, Lily thought.

The night of the party came and off Clare and Buddy drove in the green Pontiac with the top down. Lily and Hank were delighted to have a night at home alone with Dolores. After they gobbled up the quick dinner of fried rice she made from leftovers, hamburger steak, and eggs, they set about playing a game of poker. Dolores was teaching the finer points of gambling and they were in heaven, listening with rapt attention. She lit up a Camel cigarette from her hidden stash and they all took puffs.

About an hour into the game, they heard scratching noises outside. Dolores became very quiet and put her finger to her mouth as she stubbed out the cigarette in Buddy's koa ashtray.

"Shhhh! Somebody stay out there." Dolores looked excited but anxious.

*This is going to be fun*, Lily thought, her heart racing.

"Turn out da goddamned light!" said Dolores suddenly. She was worming her way along the floor to the window on her belly so no one outside could see her in the lit room.

The lights went out. In the dark they all made their way to the window. Outside the moon was bright, sending silvery shadows over the front lawn.

"Who dat?" Dolores asked in a loud, clearly excited voice.

Lily's heart was now leaping, and Hank was teetering dangerously between tears and exhilaration. This wasn't the kind of thing that ever happened in haole camp. It was one of the rules. If you were found loitering where you didn't belong, it could mean your job, or your father's.

Everything quieted outside. Then Lily saw the first flicker of light, a tiny red glow. Then there was another, and then another. She counted six red dots, the tips of burning cigarettes illuminated in the dark yard.

Dolores was getting more and more restless. Lily had never seen her quite this way.

"Eh, kids! You bettah get to your rooms." She turned, suddenly looking anxious, almost angry.

"Get to our rooms? Now?" Hank looked as if he was about to cry. *What does she mean?* thought Lily. *This is the most fun we'd had in a long time. This is like the movies.*

"Yeah, now!" Dolores's voice had changed; it was impatient and irritated. Her happy, smiling face with the rows of big teeth no longer looked quite so friendly.

"C'mon, get out of here. I don't want to hear one damn peep from you two!"

"Do-*looor*-es!" they both wailed, but she grabbed them roughly by the shoulders and pushed them to their bedrooms.

"I don't want to hear nothing from this room, or you bettah watch out!"

The doors slammed shut.

What had just happened? Why it all changed so quickly? What had happened to Dolores? Lily felt angry and betrayed by someone she'd thought was her best friend, her confidant. She lay quietly in bed and felt the warm tears streaming down her cheeks. Slowly she relaxed, and before long she was asleep.

EVERYONE WOKE SLOWLY THE NEXT MORNING. Buddy was already out "playing with his chickens," as Clare called it. He'd already staked the fighting cocks around the backyard for exercise and was busy inspecting the coops for eggs. This was usually Lily's job, but they hadn't woken her. Clare emerged only long enough to make herself a cup of black coffee and returned to the sanctuary of their bedroom.

When Lily finally made her way to the kitchen, she saw Dolores standing at the sink with her back to Lily. She was staring out the window, clearly not feeling very chipper herself.

"Howzit," she said, glancing at Lily. Her teeth flashed, but there were dark circles under her eyes, and she was holding a bottle of Coke in her hand.

"You sleep okay?"

Lily didn't bother to answer. She was still smarting from being ditched so royally the night before.

Dolores brightened after a few minutes of silence. "Hey, let's go steal some blackberries from Mrs. Foster's tree next door and make a pie." It had been their game all summer. They'd sneak into Mrs. Foster's backyard, make pockets with their T-shirts, and fill them with berries. Then Dolores would show them how to make a pie crust from scratch. In an hour, they would be filling themselves with warm pie until their mouths turned purple.

"No thanks. I'm busy," Lily said as she slammed the back door and walked outside to see if the chickens had laid any eggs. She spent the rest of the morning curled up in her room with books and movie magazines.

How could Dolores do this? Lily had thought they were friends. She'd thought they shared things. Secrets. They had read *True Confessions* and, worse, puffed on unfiltered Camels, talked and giggled about boys. But Dolores had frozen her out, probably even climbed out the window like she'd often talked about. Dolores had betrayed them, and Lily wanted to betray her right back. She headed for her mother's room.

Clare was still in bed staring straight ahead. Lily loved when she was like this. Her mother had a tendency to run about from one thing to another, rarely stopping long enough to listen. Akuhead Pupule, the Honolulu disc jockey, was coming through the radio beside Clare's bed. Lily climbed in bed with her mother, pulling the satin quilt over her knees.

"Mom, you know what Dolores did last night?" she started after a long silence, a little hesitant.

"What is it, sweetie?" Clare said, stroking Lily's cropped hair.

In a rush of words, Lily spilled it all, told her mother everything. About the boys at the theater, the *True Confessions* magazines, the smoking and gambling, the stories of Dolores's wild escapades, the climbing out her window at night. She even embellished the stories; she couldn't help herself once she got going. It made for a more dramatic case. As she talked, she felt as if she were erasing the hurt.

Clare was quiet for a long time. Then she gave Lily a hug and sent her off to Nashiwa Bakery to pick up a box of pastry and bread. The Cole's were coming over that evening for dinner.

Lily walked to the bakery, past the library, the "holy roller church," and the gym where community dances and hula recitals were held. Once there, she picked out an assortment of pastries, some with coconut on top, and *anpans*, the doughnuts filled with sweet black beans that her father loved. On the way home, she noticed Wally Perreira standing on the steps of the gym. He was skipping stones down the sidewalk when he saw Lily.

He whistled at her through his teeth, but she ignored him.

"Heh, tita. Howzit?"

Lily kept on walking, her back straight and her nose in the air, pretending not to have heard him. *He's so gross*, she thought.

When she entered their yard, she saw Lena Kamaka's station wagon pulled up under the shower tree. Her heart sank. Could it mean what she thought it did? Trouble. She couldn't be taking Dolores away, back to the detention home, could she? Lily wasn't sure if she felt more guilt or more panic.

How stupid could she have been? She'd told on Dolores because she was hurt and impulsive. She had wanted to get it off her chest. But she certainly hadn't wanted Dolores to go. She'd never expected her mother would send Dolores away. Now look what she'd done. She'd made them take her away. Lily had never been to the detention home—she didn't need to; she knew it wasn't a good place to be.

She bit her lip, but the tears began to flow again. Was there no way to stop them? *No, no, no*, she thought, feeling her desperation grow. She didn't want Dolores gone. Yes, she'd told on her, but it couldn't be *that* serious. Who would have thought Clare would call and have them come and take Dolores away? No more long talks. No more adventures exploring the camps, making sandwiches and pies. No more mischief.

"Dolores! Do-*looor*-es!" she howled, heading for the hallway that led to the maid's room. The door was ajar and the room empty. The bedding was neatly folded at the end of the bed, and her blue jeans and bright T-shirts were nowhere to be found.

Lily ran to the living room and saw her mother standing at the screen door waving. She pushed past her and ran down the front steps as Lena Kamaka backed the big station wagon out of the driveway. As she pulled ahead, Lily could see Dolores in the front seat. Her hair was still in pink curlers, tied with a bright magenta scarf, and she was chewing gum and looking straight ahead. When Dolores saw Lily coming, she looked confused for a moment as their eyes met.

Then, suddenly, a big, bright smile exploded across her face. Those big teeth glistened and she waved. In a matter of seconds, the station wagon was at the end of the block turning onto the main road.

Lily dropped to her knees on the front lawn and started to cry. This time she couldn't stop. What had she done? They'd never had a Dolores, a person who had listened to them and taken them seriously and treated them as equals, who'd made every day an adventure. Lily had caused them to take her away. It was all her fault. Her fault.

The summer ended that day, even though there were still a few weeks left until September. In the fall, Lily went back to school, this time to a new boarding school in Honolulu. She would always remember it as the last summer of her childhood. Her life was never quite the same again.

# TRUDY

Trudy Nakamura could hardly contain herself as she stood in the aisle of the plantation store. Her eyes darted back and forth trying to absorb what she saw on the shelves filled with cocoa powder, white sugar, and cake flour. She loved to bake, and it had been a long time since she'd seen ingredients like these available for just anyone to purchase. She ran her fingers over the cans and packages, remembering the impossibly flaky Napoleons and tangy apple schnitzel she had loved as a child in Germany.

It was 1948. The war and deprivation were over now. But Trudy felt her eyes filling with tears. She didn't want to make a fool of herself in such a public place. She already knew her presence in the Japanese plantation camp was causing a stir among the residents in Paia. She did stand out. She couldn't help it. Everything was different. The worst part of it was that she never seemed to do or say the right thing. She didn't have a clue how she could change that.

Her husband, Toshi, seemed quieter and distracted, no longer the funny, relaxed young soldier she'd met in Berlin. They met the day she had broken down, put her pride aside, and gone to one of the many food aid stations the U.S. Army had set up in her heavily bombed neighborhood.

That day, Trudy walked into one of the few buildings standing intact, her emotions in turmoil. She was so ashamed, but she was hungry, and, worst of all, her mother had reached a breaking point. They needed food and wood for heating.

She signed in at the desk just inside the door and moved on to folding tables stacked with coffee, canned goods, and even chocolate bars. Trudy was overwhelmed by the sight.

"Here. Take this bag," said the young soldier on the other side of the table.

She nodded, reaching automatically for it.

"We have some corned beef and Vienna sausages," he said, "although I doubt anyone in Vienna would recognize them."

Trudy looked up into a smiling face. The soldier's skin was tanned and he had the most beautiful cheekbones she had ever seen. She suspected he was Asian, but where in the world could he be from? Was this really an American soldier? Trudy tried to keep the confusion from her face.

"Try them. You'll be surprised how good they can be with a little rice and shoyu," he chuckled to himself. "But maybe I'm just a little homesick."

Homesick? The thought that an American soldier might feel homesick had never occurred to her.

She smiled back at him in spite of herself. Grateful, she picked up her bag of groceries and left. She and her mother dined better that night and in the next few days than they had in what seemed like years.

Trudy returned the next week. This time she looked for the exotic American. He was there again, handing out canned goods and laughing with his buddies, who looked a lot like him. *They must come from the same town*, she thought to herself. But where that town might be eluded her.

She was able to get rehired at the coffeehouse where she had worked during the war. It had been badly damaged, and the coffee and pastries they now served were pitiful attempts at normalcy. But Trudy was lucky to have a job, even though she wasn't sure if she would get paid.

One day, she walked up to a young man sitting alone at a corner table. He was an American soldier, something they rarely saw in the coffeehouse. But when he looked up, she recognized him immediately.

"Did you ever try that sausage no one from Vienna would ever claim?" he asked, smiling.

Trudy blushed, but she couldn't hide the fact that she was glad to see a friendly face. He began coming in regularly, sitting in the same spot in the corner and ordering just a cup of coffee. Trudy looked forward to his visits and their cheerful conversations, not sure how her fellow workers were taking the budding friendship.

One thing led to another, and within a month, Trudy realized she looked forward to her visits with this foreign man. His name was Toshi Nakamura, and he belonged to an all-Japanese-American unit that had fought its way into Germany through Sicily and Italy.

Toshi, in turn, seemed as fascinated with Trudy as she was with him. He told her he had never dreamed of spending so much time with a blonde haole woman. That was what she was, he told her: a haole. Toshi was different for her, too. She had never been one of those Germans who thought of themselves as a superior race, but she had never considered that after her husband, Franz, there could be another man in her life.

Back then, she and Toshi were full of hope for their futures. Trudy remembered how kind he had been to her, helping her with her broken English and being patient when she would lapse into the fearful, dark moods that had begun with Franz's death on the Russian front.

She was just out of school when she and had Franz met. Adolf Hitler had been the prime minister, and there had been a new optimism throughout Germany. Trudy and Franz had been too young to realize what would come next. He had joined up with the young, brown-shirted men who marched for their own futures and their country. Trudy had attended classes at the culinary school and learned to make the light, cream-filled pastries Germans were so fond of. She had dreamed of becoming a great pastry chef, and every bit of spare change she had had gone into purchasing ingredients for practicing at home.

But what had begun with so much optimism and fanfare had ended badly, and now Franz was dead. She needed to move on. She was here in Hawaii now, and Toshi was her husband. She loved Toshi, and they had so many plans for their future.

Now Trudy turned her attention back to the baking supplies on the shelves. Too much thinking about the past was never a good thing, she had discovered.

"Just look at all this stuff. I guess we know the holidays are coming."

Trudy looked over her shoulder to find a young, dark-haired woman about her age standing just behind her in front of the shelves.

"It makes me excited, too," said Trudy, smiling, aware of how her strong accent made her sound.

"I guess you're not from around here," the young woman replied. Trudy looked at an alert face with enormous brown eyes. She guessed the woman was part Hawaiian, but she wasn't familiar enough with island people yet to be able to tell.

"No. I'm from Germany. I'm new here," Trudy answered. She'd made no new friends on the plantation in the four months since she and Toshi had moved back to live with his parents. Maybe this young woman was a possible friend. She needed to practice her English, and, face it, she was lonely for someone her own age.

"Oh, you're the one everyone is talking about. Hi, my name is Clare. Clare Donahue. It's nice to meet you."

"I'm Trudy. Trudy Nakamura," she said, suddenly shy. "You may know my husband, Toshi. He's taken a job in the mill since we got back, but it's not for long. He wants to go into politics. He has so many good new ideas." Trudy knew she had disclosed way too much to a perfect stranger.

"Well, if I were you, I wouldn't tell many people around here about the politics part. There's enough talk these days about unions. They all seem to be discontented in the fields and the mill. Everyone thinks everyone else is a communist, especially the management. They're all accusing one another."

"Do you like to bake too?" asked Trudy, changing the subject and reaching for a bar of baking chocolate. She distrusted politics and thought of the evenings Toshi stayed out late with his old friends.

"Are you kidding? I love to bake. It's really the only thing I can do," said Clare. "I'm a hopeless cook. Thank God we have Dolores. She does all the cooking or we'd all starve."

There was something so cheerful and lively about Clare, it made Trudy laugh. She wanted Clare to be her friend. She needed to be around someone her own age.

"Hey, why don't we both make something and we can share the results," said Clare. "Come over to my house tomorrow afternoon. I'll make some tea and we can try each other's goodies. We'll have a regular sugar fest. We live right above the mill in Skill Village. I'll draw you a map. It will be fun." Trudy sensed Clare was as much in need of a friend as she.

Trudy felt a little guilty about spending the grocery money for luxurious baking ingredients but did it anyway. Besides, she wanted to show off a little by making something wonderful. She wasn't sure Toshi's mother was going to like this expenditure. She would consider it wasteful.

Toshi's parents had not been happy when he had brought Trudy back to Paia. She knew they had had big plans for their only son, and a German war bride was not one of them. Toshi's father, Kenji, was always polite, but he was rarely home, working long hours in the plantation machine shop. He came home in the afternoon and soaked in the family's *furo* behind their small house. After dinner, he spent his time reading the Japanese language newspapers, or visiting his friends to play cards and "talk story" about their general discontent with conditions.

Toshi's mother, Masako, was more openly hostile to her. Trudy knew her mother-in-law wished Trudy would just go away so she could have her son back. Trudy could sense she embarrassed Masako in front of her Japanese friends, with Trudy's blonde hair and foreign ways. The Hawaiian sun burned her nose and cheeks, so she took to wearing one of Toshi's straw hats on her daily walks around the camp. This called attention to her even more and seemed to anger her mother-in-law, but Masako never said anything to Trudy's face. Still, disapproval seeped from the older woman's every pore.

Trudy noticed Masako would be extra cool when she came home from working on the upcoming church bazaar at the Hongwanji temple. But this time, when Trudy arrived home with the groceries, she just ignored Masako. She was going to make her new friend cream puffs like nothing Clare had ever tasted in her life. They would not be those sodden, overly sweet pastries Masako brought home from Nashiwa Bakery.

That night after dinner, Trudy shared her fresh cream puffs with the family. Toshi and his father were delighted to have them with their coffee. Kenji smacked his lips as he finished his and gave Trudy a big smile. Even Masako took a small piece, telling Trudy she was watching her weight and that Trudy should do the same.

The next day, after helping Masako by cleaning up and doing the lunch dishes, Trudy put on her best dress—pale blue that showed off her eyes and fair skin. Toshi always loved to see her in it. She gathered the remaining cream puffs and carefully placed them in a box lined with waxed paper. The afternoon was still warm, but walking was her only way to get to Clare's house.

She placed the map Clare had drawn in her pocket and walked down to Baldwin Avenue toward the mill. The sky seemed even bluer to her, and the fragrance of her neighbor's plumeria trees cast a heady perfume in the air. As she neared Skill Village the houses became larger. The yards especially caught her attention. Most of them were shaded by large shower and monkeypod trees. Some of the homes had open, wraparound porches, and every now and then she saw a yardman pop up from behind a hibiscus hedge.

She had no difficulty finding Clare's house. It was large with white clapboard shingles on the outside and a long flight of stairs leading to the front door. Purple bougainvillea spilled onto the yard on either side of the stairway, and flowers were scattered everywhere on the lawn.

Trudy had barely knocked when she saw Clare through the screen door rushing to greet her. Clare was even prettier than she remembered. Her thick, dark brown hair tumbled to her shoulders, and her eyes seemed even larger. She wore a simple, white, sharkskin shirtdress and bare feet. It startled Trudy, who was not yet used to removing her shoes every time she entered a home.

"I'm so glad you came," Clare said as she swung open the door, and Trudy stepped into a room that was cool, inviting, and unlike any she had ever seen in her homeland. Lauhala covered glossy, painted floors, and in one corner of the living room sat two large beds. She later learned they were punees, or traditional Hawaiian beds that were used for everything from afternoon naps to accommodating visiting relatives. Clare led her to one corner of the large living room containing a rattan sofa and two matching chairs.

"Dolores! Trudy's here! Bring us some tea and that cake I made," Clare shouted to what must have been the kitchen in the back of the house. "Oh, and bring another plate for Trudy's pastries. Hell, come and join us. We're going to gossip."

Trudy was startled. She had never had a maid herself, but she knew people back in Germany who had, and they would never have considered asking the maid to join them for tea and cakes.

After a good deal of noise and banging in the kitchen, Dolores, the Donahue's newest maid, came into the living room carrying a large tray and placed it on the coffee table in front of them. On it were three cups with saucers and small plates with cutlery and napkins. Dolores was in her teens. She, too, was barefoot and wore a pair of faded jeans and a halter top.

"Oh, yum!" said Clare, biting immediately into one of Trudy's cream puffs.

Dolores had already eaten half of her pastry in one bite. Trudy sipped her tea and savored her pastry while the three laughed and talked about everything from the weather to what was new at the plantation store. What the two island woman insisted on knowing was all about Trudy. What was Germany like? Had she been frightened during the war? What were she and Toshi going to do next? Where would they live?

For the first time since arriving here, except when she was alone at night with Toshi, Trudy relaxed and spoke freely. Clare and Dolores hung on her every word, curious about everything.

The afternoon flew by and was filled with so much laughter and so many treats that Trudy was sure she wouldn't be able to eat her dinner. Clare's coconut cake had been light and airy, as delicious as her own cream puffs.

At four o'clock, the mill whistle blew and startled them. Trudy knew she had to rush and get back to the house before Toshi came home, and Clare and Dolores had to get ready for the children's round of baths, dinner, and bedtime stories. They all agreed to repeat the afternoon's activities again soon.

On her walk home, Trudy realized she felt lighter than she had since she had been on the island. Toshi was waiting for her when she arrived. His face wore a devilish grin, something she hadn't seen in a while.

"Why don't you go inside and freshen up," he said. "I've got the car tonight, and I'm taking you to Wailuku for dinner."

Trudy was already wearing her best dress, so she ran a comb through her hair, wiped the perspiration from her brow, and applied fresh lipstick. They rode to Wailuku together in Kenji's old Dodge, feeling hopeful and young again.

Over dinner, they talked about their future, and Toshi leaned across the table to hold her hand. He wanted to go into politics, he told her, to change the way things were done on the plantation and in Hawaii. He was making plans to run for public office in the fall. He hinted that he was worried about Kenji's frustration with work; he feared his father felt trapped and desperate.

Trudy told him about her day and that she someday wanted to start her own baking business. That night in their small room, they fell into each other's arms, happy and certain their lives were about to change.

TOSHI SPENT THE NEXT FEW MONTHS working on his election campaign, having banners and cards bearing his picture printed and refining his political platform. He showed up at every social occasion in Paia and made the rounds, shaking hands and encouraging people to stand up for better working conditions. He was getting noticed by people, and although they seemed a little nervous about his bold ideas, he thrilled them every time he spoke.

Trudy was proud of Toshi and talked enthusiastically about him with Clare in what had become a weekly afternoon tea. The three began planning other activities. Several times they took sandwiches and cold drinks to the beach at Baldwin Park. They'd share their meals and tan their legs in the warm sun, happy to not be lonely for the company of women.

But as the election drew near, Trudy began to notice Kenji becoming increasingly quieter. Her father-in-law barely spoke to her anymore, and he and Toshi argued, just out of range of her hearing, when they stepped outside to smoke. When she asked Toshi about it, he told her it was nothing, that his father was getting some crazy ideas. Still, she could feel the tension around their small house building. Trudy hoped it had nothing to do with her.

Masako, too, was more guarded. *Maybe she thinks I will say something when I go down to Skill Village,* Trudy thought. But she wasn't sure what she could say. She knew very little, only that tensions seemed to be rising at the mill and in the fields. Workers had been hurt with some new machinery, and many believed management was not listening to them about the dangers. Some of the field workers were growing more vocal about their low pay and poor working conditions, too.

Momentum built all summer for Toshi's candidacy on the Democratic ticket. In late September, he survived the primary election, and his name went on the ballot for the general election in early November. He and Trudy spoke excitedly about the possibility of moving to Honolulu should he be elected to the territorial legislature. They were so wrapped up in each other they barely noticed Kenji and Masako anymore and spent most of their evenings away campaigning.

On Halloween, Clare and her husband, Buddy, who held a management-level job in the plantation main office, invited them to a costume party at their house. Trudy was delighted. Toshi seemed happy, too; he liked Buddy, who had helped him get his campaign materials together and had introduced him to some important people already holding public office.

That night they borrowed Kenji's car and drove to Buddy and Clare's wearing costumes from *The Mikado*. Their costumes had been entirely Trudy's idea. Kenji took one look at them before they left and grunted. Trudy got the feeling he wasn't completely thrilled with them. But he didn't say anything. What good would it do? They were already on their way.

When they arrived, they found the Donahue house completely transformed. Black and orange crepe-paper streamers hung from the ceiling and balloons filled the house. The house lights had been dimmed with red light bulbs, and Tommy Dorsey and Sarah Vaughan could be heard on the phonograph console in the living room.

Dolores, dressed in black with a white apron, looked awkward as she passed hors d'oeuvres resembling eyeballs and dismembered fingers. On the porch, Trudy noticed grownups dunking for apples in a large, galvanized tub. They were going to need a drink for all this, she thought. Everyone else seemed to have had a head start with the booze.

The night wore on and Trudy caught a glimpse of Toshi across the room talking with some of the men from Buddy's office. He looked as if he was having a good time. She loved him so much.

At about nine o'clock, the phone rang and Dolores called Buddy into another room to take it. He was gone just a few minutes, and when he returned all gaiety had left his face. He headed straight for Toshi and pulled him back into the other room.

When Toshi emerged, he was ashen. He headed for Trudy and took her arm almost roughly, walking her directly to the door. They got into the car without so much as a word.

"It's Dad. I've got to go," he eventually told Trudy, seeing the worried look on her face. "There's a big cane fire near Maliko Gulch and maybe another one down at the mill."

When they got home, he changed into work clothes and prepared to leave. "I know we don't normally lock the doors, Trudy, but lock them tonight and stay inside," he instructed her before leaving. "Make sure my mother stays in, too."

Trudy knew not to ask for more information, so she kept quiet, knowing he would tell her about it later. She could hear the fire engines wailing now, and lights began turning on all up and down their street. Masako was holed up in her room, which seemed dark, so Trudy sat in the living room alone and waited. After midnight, she fell asleep on the sofa.

It was morning before Toshi arrived home, covered with soot and more tired than she had ever seen him. He went out into the washhouse to bathe while she made an omelet and leftover fried rice for him. Masako obviously hadn't slept at all either, and Trudy gently convinced her to go back to bed. There was no Kenji.

"Dad's missing," Toshi said, sitting down to eat breakfast. "I'm really worried." Quietly, he confided to Trudy about trouble his father had been getting into with the new boss in the mill's machine shop. Anger had been building for some time, and now Toshi was afraid some of the workers had taken things into their own hands in an attempt to teach management a lesson.

The machine shop had been vandalized and four fields set ablaze; the fire had burned so hot the flames and smoke could be seen all the way to Kihei on one end of the island and Haiku on the other. But no one had seen Kenji.

In the following days, workers began cleaning up the debris and got the machine shop up and running. Field hands went into the burned fields to see if they could salvage any of the cane. It was hopeless, they realized, and instead they cleared the fields.

On the second day, they found Kenji. He had been in the field the night the fires started. There was little doubt he had been one of the men who'd started them. He had apparently slipped into an irrigation ditch by accident and broken his leg. He likely had lain there unable to run, and he had not been found sooner because burned cane had covered the ditch.

Masako was stoic when she heard the news. She stood silently, then simply nodded her head. Toshi went over to his mother, put his arm gently around her frail shoulders, and walked her into the room she and his father had shared.

Trudy did all the cooking and household chores for the next few days, to make sure Masako rested. Meanwhile, Toshi spent his days at the plantation office trying to straighten out matters so Masako wouldn't be evicted from the camp house and left destitute. With Buddy's help, the plantation manager softened and agreed to let her stay as long as she wanted; he even released Kenji's small retirement pay.

Kenji's funeral service was held at the Paia Hongwanji. Trudy had never attended a Buddhist funeral, and she listened carefully to instructions from Masako's friends. What seemed like the entire population of the Japanese camp arrived, the men in somber black suits and the women in black dresses, some with Buddhist rosaries. Following the services, Kenji was buried in the graveyard near the temple. A shiny black marker bearing his name in Japanese characters, or *kanji*, would be placed above it.

ON THE DAY OF THE ISLAND-WIDE elections, Toshi and Trudy dressed and took the car to Wailuku to wait for election returns at the Democratic headquarters. They picked up Buddy and Clare on the way, and the four made plans for dinner in the palm-filled courtyard of the Wailuku Grand Hotel.

The ballots had all finally been counted near midnight, and Toshi had won by a landslide. Everyone proclaimed he was the new hope for the party. Trudy was so proud of him. On the ride home, she slid over next to him, putting her head on his shoulder,

In the next two months, they made plans to move to Honolulu during the legislative session. Toshi was granted a leave from his job at the mill, even though the local newspaper had been running editorials suggesting that he had ties to suspicious labor leaders, who might in turn have ties to the Communist Party. Thank God the plantation manager seemed to have more sense than to listen to rumors, thought Trudy.

Masako chose to stay on Maui near her friends and neighbors and not to accompany the two to the city. Trudy was secretly happy to have Toshi all to herself.

The most difficult part about leaving Maui saying goodbye to Clare and Dolores. The three had laughed, shared meals, and solved the problems of the world. She knew her time with them had eased her transition to a new life with Toshi. The three made promises to write and keep in touch, even though they all knew things would never be quite the same.

Toshi was going far, everyone could see it. He would be one of those men who helped make Hawaii into a different sort of place, and Trudy would go there with him. She was sure of that.

# THE DOCTOR

Maggie Sullivan, the nurse just getting off ward duty, stormed into Dr. Donahue's small, untidy office at the back of the plantation hospital. That rambling, one-story wooden structure sat on a lawn shaded by vast monkeypod trees, which had been planted years earlier by the nature-loving wife of a long-forgotten plantation manager and provided a certain serenity to the place.

"I've had it," Nurse Sullivan said, her hands on her ample hips. "That Antone Jacinto has got to stop sleeping off his drunken binges in our hospital beds. This is the second time this week, and I'm sick, sick, sick of it." Just shy of stomping her feet, she tried to keep her voice under control.

Dr. Donahue looked up from the stack of medical records he was updating. A man of about sixty, he had spent much of his life following his whims, working in places that had fascinated him, staying for a few years and then moving on. When he had been a young physician, he'd escorted the bones of Chinese workers in large ceramic crocks from the Pacific Northwest back to their families in San Francisco. Now, as chief of surgery in this small plantation hospital in Upcountry Maui, he confessed to a hunger for adventure and a wanderlust that kept him moving. This weakness ensured that in spite of his formidable surgical skills, he would never become as rich or famous as his dear Irish mother had dreamed.

His wife, Mrs. Donahue, an offspring of missionaries, cared very little that the good doctor's career had stuck. In the early days of their marriage, she'd been too busy trying to keep their brood of five boys from killing each other. When they were finally gone, she turned her attention to good works and shopping in San Francisco whenever she could tear herself from her bridge and mahjong games.

The hospital grounds were surrounded by cane fields, and in the months before the cane was harvested, when the fields were burned to clear the rubbish and rats, it was all he could do to keep the sprawling wooden structure free of charred debris that covered the cement walkways and the roof and threatened every room in the hospital.

He pushed his glasses onto his head and stared at Nurse Sullivan for a moment. He had a soft spot for the competent nurse. Her skills were beyond reproach, but it was her normally good-natured demeanor that reminded him of the Irish women in his neighborhood growing up. It had always made him feel good just to be around them.

"Humph!" he said.

"You've got to do something, Dr. Donahue," she said in something close to a whine. "He gets drunk and won't go home. His wife's Rosa Jacinto, the bus driver at Holy Rosary School. The big one. He's scared to death of her."

"I would be too," Dr. Donahue said under his breath. "Okay, let me think about it."

Nurse Sullivan didn't look satisfied, but she turned on her heel and left the office. He knew he was going to have to put a stop to Jacinto's nocturnal visits. Nurse Sullivan had been at the hospital for two years and was nearing the end of her contract. She was the best nurse he'd ever worked with, and he wanted to keep her on for another two at least. *She should have been a doctor*, he thought to himself. But, in 1939, it wasn't easy for a woman. He valued her consistency and sensed a passionate nature beneath all that bluster and efficiency.

Dr. Donahue was a man of few words and one of the best physicians the hospital had ever had. He would travel miles to deliver a baby on a kitchen table, and he never complained when he was woken in the night to attend to a worker whose arm had been caught in a roller at the mill. He also harbored a wicked sense of humor that bordered on the diabolical. He'd once scrawled the word "slacker" in pink, antibacterial mercurochrome across the backside of a field worker trying to fake yet another injury.

His impatience with idle conversation and indifference to social skills sometimes kept him from being included in the plantation's tight haole social circle. He preferred it that way. Much happier playing poker and drinking single-malt scotch with the Catholic priests, he didn't miss the cocktail parties full of empty talk.

The doctor made his way down the hall past the surgery. He peered inside, noticing that the bottle of holy water he always kept on a ledge near the operating table, for Catholic patients near death, was almost empty. He would have to take it to Father O'Brien and get it refilled when they met for their weekly poker, he thought. He wasn't sure whether it made his patients feel better or worse to have it there.

After one night of drinking and cards with the congenial priests, he'd impulsively promised his youngest son to the church. His wife, being a descendant of Protestant missionaries, had not been amused when he'd marched the reluctant boy to Holy Rosary Church the next Saturday morning to be baptized, thereby fulfilling his promise.

"Jacinto, you dirty bugger!" the doctor hollered as he entered the ward.

The mill mechanic was not looking at all well this morning. Above his right eye was a cut, and blood had coagulated and hardened on his puffy brow. He looked as if he were about to lose the breakfast of eggs and toast with guava jelly he'd been served before being found out.

"Aww, I stay some sorry, Docta," he said. "Pacheco and I wen tie one on down at Lita's last night. Sumbitch. Rosa goin be some pissed." He sat up and pulled on his cotton aloha shirt, then struggled to put big feet into his special occasion shoes.

"You gotta stop coming into the surgical ward to sleep it off, Jacinto," the doctor said, handing him a comb one of the nurses had brought for him to use. "I don't care what Rosa does to you; you're scaring the nurses and making more work for them. Next time you do this, I'm going to actually operate on you. Take out that useless appendix of yours."

Jacinto straightened up. "Aw, Doc. You wouldn't do dat, would you? What I wen do was so bad?"

"Jacinto, you listen to me."

"Okay, okay, I get it. Nevah again. Okay?"

He pulled on his pants and unsteadily headed for the door, giving Dr. Donahue a friendly pat on the shoulder as he passed, still smelling of stale alcohol.

ON SATURDAYS, THE CLINIC WAS ONLY open until noon, and when the last patient had left, Dr. Donahue locked the drug cabinet and grabbed his black medical bag. It was a great day to spend in his garden, he thought as he headed for his old Packard. He decided to enjoy the sun and cooler weather and take the long way home, down through the camps, past the gas station and the company store, to lower Paia. From there he drove along the ocean, past Hookipa, with its crashing winter swell, and then veered up into the cane fields through a tunnel of trees. The trees, like the ones at the hospital, had been planted years ago by the same plantation manager's wife and her friends in an effort to beautify the island, and they had succeeded. Now tunnels of shade trees lined many of the main roads.

When he reached Hamakuapoko, he decided not to stop and check for mail at the post office. Instead, he turned at the corner and headed down a dirt road past large homes with verandas, clipped green lawns, and brilliant shower trees scattering blossoms and pods on the ground. Before the end of the street he turned into his own driveway. His wife's car was gone.

"Hey, Yoko," he yelled as he entered through the screened kitchen door. He saw she already had a banana pie in the pie safe for after dinner. Maybe he could steal a piece before lunch. Yoko knew he had a mean sweet tooth.

She turned from sink where she was shelling peas. "Eh, Docta! How you? You hungry?"

"Starving," he said. He loved when his wife was gone and Yoko would make him one of her stir-fried dishes with leftover rice. Yoko and her husband, Hiroshi, had worked for the family since the Donahues' youngest son, Buddy, was born. They lived in a small house behind the main house near the garden. Buddy was more attached to her than to his own mother.

Yoko began chopping leftover pork, green onions, and mushrooms.

"Hey, Yoko. You know this guy Jacinto from the Paia mill?" He wasn't sure why he'd asked her. He just wanted to talk to someone and get this latest problem off his mind.

"I don't think so. Why?" she answered, dropping pieces of pork into hot peanut oil in the wok and watching it sizzle.

Dr. Donahue proceeded to tell her about his problem.

"Oh, hell! Jus' cut him and sew him up! That oughta teach dat Portagee a lesson!" Yoko was not one for mincing words. She had a big heart, but he knew Hiroshi was scared to death of her. It seemed to him a lot of men were terrified of their wives.

She placed a steaming plate of food in front of him and returned to the sink to shell peas. He decided not to press her. Instead, he dug his fork into the fragrant plate in front of him.

THE NEXT WEEK AT THE HOSPITAL turned out to be a busy one. On Tuesday, a train approaching the mill had been going too fast, and the engineer attempting to brake at the last minute had managed to flip it on its side, badly injuring both his assistant and several men near the tracks. As a result, Dr. Donahue had been in surgery more that week than usual. By Friday night, he was exhausted and happy to get home to his dinner, followed by a cigar and brandy.

He had no sooner settled into bed after listening to the late news on the radio when the phone began ringing. It was Nurse Sullivan on the other end. She'd had a long week, too, and was in no mood for any more trouble.

"He's here again!" she screamed into the phone. "You've got to do something; I can't take him anymore." Worn out, she was dangerously near tears.

"Okay, okay. Hold your horses. I'll be right there," he said reluctantly. He threw on his rumpled clothes, grabbed his medical bag, and headed outside to the Packard. When he drove up to the hospital, Nurse Sullivan was pacing at the front door, her arms crossed against her chest.

"Honestly, Dr. Donahue. I can't take this anymore. This time he cut himself a way in through the window screen and urinated all over the floor in the hallway. He's this way." She led him into the surgical ward, where Jacinto was half asleep, curled into a fetal position, drunkenly humming to himself, a stupid grin on his face.

"Well, at least he's not belligerent," he said, turning to meet the furious nurse's eyes. He could see she wasn't having any of his humor tonight."

"All right, get the surgery ready."

She stood still and looked at him, surprised and questioning, unsure whether she'd heard him correctly. Did he really mean it? He was going to actually operate? She slowly turned and walked out of the room toward the surgery.

It had been just the three of them in the surgery that night. Dr. Donahue knew what he was doing was hardly orthodox, but what the hell. This place, the plantation, was like the Wild West anyway. People made their own rules on these neighbor island plantations. Incompetence and drunkenness were tolerated at the top. Labor conditions of overworked, underpaid workers were regularly ignored. He had a hospital to run, and that hospital needed to keep good nurses.

Nurse Sullivan remained silent as he stitched up Jacinto. She tried not to look directly at the doctor. Knowing she might have pushed him to this, she felt guiltier than she should. The doctor, after all, hadn't actually operated on Jacinto. His appendix was still intact. The incision was barely more than a scratch, but it would be enough to scare him silly when he finally woke.

"Not a word," he said to her as they wheeled the patient back to the ward. She nodded silently, then followed him back to his office.

"Well, that should cure him of his habit," he said, putting on his jacket and grabbing his bag, leaving Nurse Sullivan staring silently after him. He jumped into the Packard, still parked in front of the hospital. It was now close to one a.m.

*I think I'll take the long way,* he thought. *The full moon will be lovely on the water tonight.* Down the hill he drove again, past the mill and through Paia, until he reached the bluff above Hookipa Beach. Here he pulled off the road and watched the waves crash on the reef. After a few minutes, he grew tired and started the engine again, heading toward the tunnel of trees on his way home. Maybe Yoko had left the rest of the banana pie in the pie safe. He was suddenly ravenous.

# VERONICA

Veronica Caldwell flew into town on a stormy Christmas Eve in 1954. It was one of those muggy days local people called *kona*. She tried to shield her two children, all pink-cheeked and windblown blondness, from the needles of rain pelting them as they ran for the long, flat terminal.

She saw him right away. Her husband. There behind the chain-link fence near baggage claim stood Frank Caldwell, tall and reed thin, his heart bursting with anticipation. It had been three months since he'd flown to Maui to take over the laboratory at Central Maui Sugar.

Part of Frank was just simply relieved she'd come. He wasn't sure she would. Veronica was never happy in the remote locations his profession took him. But he kept on hoping. He'd rented a sprawling house on the beach at Spreckelsville. It was modest by management standards—built by plantation carpenters with Canac ceilings made from sugar cane by-products. The floors throughout the house were a hard, black, polished concrete, perfect for wet, sandy feet and the occasional tsunami. He'd hired Hattie Carvalho, the wife of the mill foreman, to come in three times a week to clean and cook. Hattie was a talker, but no one could bake bread or deliver a fragrant, vinegary *vinha d'ahlos* like she could. Frank was pleased. Now it was up to Veronica to make an effort to adjust.

The proximity of the house to the Maui Country Club was what appealed to him most. Veronica could make friends with the other plantation wives, and the children could play in the pool and on the tennis courts. He had done his best to make it attractive for his perpetually discontented wife.

The children ran squealing to him. Heidi, with her short, mopsy curls, and Frank Junior, whom everyone called Chip and who was often prone to moods now that he approached his twelfth birthday, excitedly told him about their trip. Veronica stood back, as pretty as he'd remembered. She'd done something different with her hair; a thick, blond streak now ran from the top of her head to her chin. She'd cut it differently, too, into a fashionable bob. Frank took all this in the second before he enveloped her in his arms and breathed in a heady aroma of shampoo and *L'Air du Temps.*

They'd met at Texas A&M in the spring semester of his senior year, and she had been the loveliest creature he'd ever laid his eyes on, sassy and flirtatious. He'd been surprised she would even go out with him. Frank was pleasant-looking enough, but his friends said he was too serious, always studying. Looking at him from behind reminded you of a bird, all long neck and skinny legs. His brilliance saved him in the science lab, where he could be funny and just plain easy to be around.

At nineteen, Veronica was well on her way to recreating herself. The toss of her chin-length brown hair, the pastel sweater sets and pearls, a coppery tan acquired on the lawn in spring term—all hinted she came from money. But there was no money anywhere. Veronica scrubbed floors and waited tables at Ruby's Diner outside Amarillo all summer to afford college. There was no way she was going to stay in that hole of a West Texas town. Let's face it, her family was piss poor—her mother, fat and angry all the time; her father, drunk at The Blue Spot from Friday to Sunday morning when the three of them dressed in starched clothes and headed for Awake Baptist Church to declare their love of the Lord and promise abstinence.

Veronica knew there was more. She had seen it in the movies at the Metro and read about how beautiful people lived in New York and Hollywood. So she held her feelings close and made her plans of escape. She never listened to her mother saying she was too good for the town, for them. Veronica tore a picture of Rita Hayworth out of a movie magazine she found at the hairdresser and clipped it to the mirror above her dresser. Rita Hayworth had married a prince. She could, too, couldn't she?

Frank Caldwell was hardly the prince she'd imagined, but in Veronica's third year of college, she'd become tired of pretending, tired of summers of drudgery, heat, dust, and boredom, of waiting for her life to begin. Frank was a nice man and smart. She had no doubt he'd go far in life, and she could go with him. It wasn't that she was cold-blooded. Veronica liked him a lot, but, more importantly, he was head over heels in love with her.

They married in the living room of the Caldwell family home in Palo Alto, California, the summer after Frank graduated. Frank's friends from his private high school and his parents' friends from the local golf club were all at the wedding. Veronica decided not to invite her parents, Bobby and Eula, and instead sent them a telegram right after the ceremony telling them how sudden all of this had been and how ecstatic she was to be married to such a nice, promising young man. They responded by sending a set of crocheted antimacassars her mother had made to be used as head rests on living room chairs. They went out in the next bag Veronica donated to the Salvation Army.

Veronica loved Frank's family. Books lined the walls of rooms in the house—books they'd actually read and discussed over drinks before dinner. Frank's father, Colin, headed up the chemistry department at Stanford, and his mother, Cynthia, gave teas and luncheons for faculty wives. One Wednesday each month, she attended garden club meetings in the hall of the Episcopal church. Veronica especially liked that they talked at the dinner table. There were lively, interesting conversations she could join without the long silences she had endured at her own family's table. Colin and Cynthia listened to her ideas and laughed at her jokes. She felt intelligent and valued. In a strange way, it warmed her to Frank even more.

Frank's mother, surprised at how little Veronica knew about entertaining, taught her to set a proper table, getting the napkins and silver to line up just right, making the tea with just the right amount of fresh mint, and ordering traditional, buttery scones from the town's fanciest bakery. Veronica listened and followed faithfully. She loved her mother-in-law. When Cynthia asked about Eula, Veronica's answers were vague. Her mother held a very important job in their county, Veronica said. She didn't have much time for teas. She wondered if Cynthia guessed at her modest beginnings. She must have suspected but was kind enough not to pry.

In the months before Frank was offered his first position supervising the mill operations on a sugar plantation in Jamaica, Cynthia and Veronica spent every other Wednesday in San Francisco shopping at I. Magnin & Co. and having lunch at Blum's next door before taking in one of the Broadway road shows at the Geary Theater. Veronica was happier than she'd ever imagined she could be. Every night she lay close to Frank in the spare upstairs bedroom and knew her real life had begun. When he reached for her, she went to him eagerly, letting his hands move from her breasts to the soft spot between her legs.

Riding now to Spreckelsville in the new Chevrolet, with Frank driving beside her and the children excited in the back seat, Veronica wondered where the years had gone. It was more than a decade now since his first position in Jamaica. Then there was the year spent in Cuba on another sugar plantation. A horrible year, she remembered, when she slept with a squirt gun filled with Clorox in case of intruders. Unrest was everywhere as guerilla groups joined peasant sympathizers in the mountains, opposing President Batista. They all sensed it was only a matter of time before the entire political and economic structure collapsed. Within months after they left, it did. Thank God Hawaii wasn't like that. Everything would be different here. *Please*, she thought, *let me be different, too.*

VERONICA WOKE TO THE SOUND OF gentle waves on the beach in front of the house. Streaks of sunlight through the squat Samoan coconut trees outside the bedroom window made patterns on the lawn. The coarse grass stretched to a tangle of *naupaka* vines creeping along the sand, creating a barrier to the beach. She lay quietly looking out the window. She'd slept so soundly she hadn't heard Frank get up, dress, and leave. From a far corner of the house, she could hear Heidi's chirpy chatter and Chip's adolescent mumble. Freshly baked biscuits and bacon, smells that made any Southern girl think all was right with the world, made their way into the room.

She rolled onto her side, stared absently, then got out of bed and made her way to the bathroom for a glass of water. In the mirror, Veronica noticed the tiredness and deep furrows of the night before were gone from her face. She looked positively dewy. *New dawn, new me*, she thought to herself, grabbing her bathrobe and starting for the kitchen and coffee.

"Oh, look. The missus is up," said Hattie, who had already fed the children and was regaling them with stories of adventures to be had on Maui, volcanoes to scale and swinging bridges to cross. You could see Hattie Carvalho had been lovely in her youth, but her six children and hard plantation life had taken their toll. About her was an aura of warmth, caring, and toughness. What was missing was a sense of disappointment of the sort Veronica felt. Hattie's once-dark hair was now threaded with gray, and tight curls courtesy of a Toni Home Permanent encircled her head. Here was a survivor, one whose very being still was filled with an overload of joy and vinegar. Unlike Veronica, Hattie's life had gone as she'd always knew it would, and she was fine with it.

"Aiye, Miz Caldwell, you some good-looking *wahine*. No wonder your husband been miss you. Come sit here and I get you one cup coffee."

"Thank you, Hattie. Frank says you're indispensable, and I can see the children are already yours."

"We going make pies this morning, and then I going home for make dinner for my family. I put you guys' dinner in the ice box. All you going do is heat 'em up. I wen tell Mr. Caldwell already. He wen to da office for check something. He be back by noon." Hattie was standing with her back to Veronica cutting a ripe papaya and scraping the black seeds into a plastic container to save for the pigs. Nothing on the plantation was wasted.

Veronica had almost forgotten in all the moving and excitement that this was Christmas Day. She remembered the children's unwrapped gifts in one of her suitcases.

"Oh, Hattie, you're an angel. I can already see I'm going to need a little guidance from you." She had just met the woman but felt an immediate and sincere affection for her.

After breakfast, Veronica retired to the bedroom to dress and wrap the gifts she'd bought in San Francisco, leaving the kids in the kitchen with Hattie, happily rolling dough and fitting it into pie tins. Even Chip seemed to be getting into the spirit. Veronica hadn't felt this happy in a very long time. Maui would be good to them. Frank would be home soon, they'd have Christmas dinner early, open gifts, and maybe take a ride to get a better look at the island.

IN THE DAYS AND WEEKS THAT followed, Veronica threw herself into her new life. She got the children registered in Kaunoa School, the English Standard School nearby where, though it was public, students were required to speak proper English for admission, not the pidgin spoken in the plantation camps. The classes were racially diverse in spite of the not-so-subtle intent. The Chinese, Japanese, and part-Hawaiian children of business leaders, professionals, and teachers made up half the student body.

Veronica and Frank were invited to cocktails and dinner in the homes of other plantation families like their own that made up the island hierarchy. Veronica soon saw the real authority on the island lay with the Upcountry set, the handful belonging to, or married into, Hawaii's missionary families. While the two groups, the newly arrived plantation families and the *kamaaina,* appeared to outsiders to be the same, within that closed society the differences were clearly apparent. It had to do with their deep connection to the land itself and its history.

It was at one of these Upcountry cocktail parties where Veronica met Glenda Preston, sister of the plantation manager, Harold Balding. Glenda and Harold's great-grandfather had been a confidant of King Kalakaua, but in the revolution against Kalakaua's sister, Queen Liliuokalani, their ancestor had sided with the American contingent. Later, when the Republic was formed, he and other businessmen in the sugar industry had carte blanche to run Hawaii as they chose. Harold and Glenda's parents raised the two of them in Honolulu and on the Big Island, where their mother's family owned a cattle ranch.

Glenda and Harold attended Punahou School, after which he had gone on to Yale and she to Bennington College. But country life was not for Glenda. Her tastes ran to lunches with a select group of old school friends—lunches that often stretched into the cocktail hour and beyond. For all her refined tastes, Glenda was a slut when it came to getting close to celebrities and money. She could often be found at the bar at the Royal Hawaiian when it was rumored Doris Duke or Bing Crosby was in town. This partially explained the fact that she now had two divorces behind her, making her more than a bit racy in her social set.

Veronica and Frank had arrived a little late at Harold Balding's home above Makawao. Veronica liked to make an entrance and not appear too eager, a tactic that made Frank uneasy since Harold was his boss. The house, unlike many kamaaina homes, was low and modern, designed by one of the newer island architects. Vladimir Ossipoff, a Russian by birth, had an international style that borrowed liberally from Japanese design, with long lanais and sliding screen doors. Party guests were already gathered for the sunset on the lanai facing the valley below.

"Oh, there you two are." It was Sarah Balding, Harold's often aloof, long-suffering wife. From the moment Sarah met Harold at Punahou, he had been the only one for her. Unfortunately, rumor had it Harold was a bit too interested in the young Filipino boys coming of age in the camps.

"There are so many people dying to meet your young wife, Frank." Sarah had Veronica by the hand and led her through the living room, with its mixture of low-slung teak furniture, oriental rugs, and heirlooms. "Of course, you must meet Harold's sister, Glenda here, from Honolulu. She always livens up the place."

They found Glenda on the lanai wearing a formfitting, strapless cocktail dress, in spite of the nippy Upcountry evening, and surrounded by three of Harold's plantation supervisors. She held court, as she always did, with raucous tales of her misdeeds and embarrassments, making herself the butt of her own jokes. The men were clearly delighted with her ribald humor, egging her to tell even more.

The laughter stopped as Sarah and Veronica approached.

"Ah, a fresh face in our midst!" Glenda looked Veronica up and down with an amused half smile.

"I see you're your charming self tonight, Glenda," said Sarah. You could see she wanted to say something more but thought better of it.

"I've heard so much about you." Veronica offered her hand, which Glenda ignored and instead leaned in and gave her an air kiss on her cheek.

"Now, you must excuse me, boys. I need to get to know the new competition on the island." Glenda took Veronica by the elbow and steered her to the bar, where she took it upon herself to order Veronica a mai tai.

"You've heard about these, I'm sure, but watch out, they can pack a real kick."

"Thanks for the warning." Veronica was being led to a corner of the deep lanai, which was filled with several rattan chairs and a large punee backed with pillows.

"Don't sit there," said Glenda, pointing to the punee. "It's seen way too much action. Some of which was my own, I'm delighted to report."

"Hmmm, I suppose we could all use a little of that once in a while," Veronica laughed. She felt herself warming to Glenda, recognizing the same restlessness she often felt but tried to keep neatly under wraps.

"Frank's a darling, isn't he? I'm afraid he isn't my type. Not nearly bad enough. How're you liking being on our little island?" Glenda reached for a cigarette in a small silver cup on the coffee table. "Finding anything to do besides getting swacked on weekends? There's way too much drinking here, you know. Of course, I'm right in there with them. But believe me, I watch it when I'm home. Terrible for the looks. Don't get caught up in it, honey."

"Oh, don't worry about me. I've lived on enough islands to know better. I'd like to know I still have a future."

"Bored already, aren't you? Listen, get someone to watch the kids and come stay with me out at Diamond Head. It'll do you some good. I could use the company, and I'd love to show you off at the Outrigger. You can meet some new friends and have a few laughs. It'll perk you up. Get your mind off the monotony."

"I'll give it some thought and talk to Frank." Veronica felt a strange combination of excitement and fear. She'd already made a promise to herself to try to be more contented, to concentrate on being a better wife and mother this time around. But she was drawn to Glenda's offer and would think about it.

IT TOOK HER EXACTLY TWO WEEKS to decide to join Glenda. Frank seemed happy she was going, even though he balked a bit when she first told him.

"It's only for a weekend, Frank. I've never really been to Honolulu other than our stopover coming here."

"Watch out for her, Veronica. Glenda's charming and fun, but she seems to court disaster." Frank looked worried and Veronica wanted to soothe his fears. She loved this man for his steadiness and goodness. But being in another outpost, far from the world she craved, kept eating at her, disturbing her sleep and her days.

"I will, you silly man. Stop worrying about me. Hattie's got the kids taken care of, and you can even take off to Makena to fish."

The following weekend, Veronica boarded Hawaiian Airlines for Honolulu. Flying over the island, she first saw Diamond Head, green from the recent rainy spell, then two big hotels, one of them Pepto-Bismol pink, a jumble of low-rise houses and buildings, and then the small airport next to a shallow, turquoise lagoon. Honolulu was hardly San Francisco, she thought. Glenda was at the gate in an Alfred Shaheen "poi pounder" pants set that was all the rage these days, holding three strands of sweet-smelling *pikake* leis.

"I'm so glad you could come, my dear. I can't wait for you to meet my friends, and they're dying to meet you. We'll stop at the Outrigger for a drink first. You can survey the landscape, if you know what I mean. Then we'll head home and change for dinner. I've booked the Monarch Room at the Royal. You'll love it. It's so over the top, like something from *The Arabian Nights*. I know it sounds garish, but everyone stays there."

THE OUTRIGGER CANOE CLUB WAS LIKE nothing Veronica had imagined. It was hard for her to understand at first why it seemed important in so many people's lives. The entrance to the low structure was in the middle of a shopping arcade between the Royal Hawaiian and the Moana Hotels. Inside the dim interior, Glenda seemed to know everyone, many of whom looked like they'd just come in from surfing or paddling. Everyone was tanned, half of them barefoot with T-shirts pulled over damp swim shorts. Veronica thought she'd never seen so many sandy, sunburned bodies in her life.

When they stepped onto the covered lanai beside the ocean, she understood its appeal immediately. The white sand beach stretched on one side past the Moana to a breakwater, and Diamond Head stood in the distance. On her right, the Royal had roped off a prime area of the public beach for the exclusive use of its guests. Straight ahead was the most benign, pristine beach she'd seen in Hawaii. She expected Olympic champion Duke Kahanamoku to emerge from the surf at any moment.

Veronica felt something new and different happening inside herself. Everything about Honolulu so far seemed open compared to the tightly regulated plantation life she'd been living on Maui. She felt as if she could breathe. "Don't you just love this place?" said Glenda, after she'd ordered two mai tais from Charlie, the bartender.

The following evening, Veronica dressed for dinner at the Monarch Room. They'd cancelled their reservations the night before after the second mai tai, when the bar filled with Friday night regulars. Glenda knew everyone and clearly loved having someone new to bring to the familiar crowd. By the end of the evening, Veronica's shoes had come off, and she was dancing a bad hula in a club they'd made their way to, down Kalakaua Avenue. She didn't try to explain it to herself, but she felt young again. This time without the painful urgency to move beyond her origins, beyond West Texas, beyond Bobby and Eula.

VERONICA PUT ON THE DRESS SHE had packed for dinner. Glenda took one look at her and said, "Too many small islands, darling," before heading for her own closet. She returned with a short black dress made of silk with thin spaghetti straps and a pair of gold sandals.

"Try this on. You'll be smashing with that hair and those long legs of yours."

Embarrassed, Veronica tried on the dress. It fit perfectly. When she turned to look at herself in the mirror, she had to try hard to keep from laughing out loud. That simple dress transformed her into a sophisticated woman of the world. It made her look like the woman she tried to be but never quite achieved becoming.

"Enough of that 'Texas pretty' nonsense, Sweetie. We's goin' lookin' for bigger game." The remark made Veronica uneasy. She struggled to contain herself and not seem like the hillbilly she was afraid she might still be. They left the house in Glenda's little red MG convertible and made their way around Diamond Head, down Kalakaua Avenue to the Royal Hawaiian.

The grounds of the hotel began on Kalakaua Avenue, where neatly trimmed coconut palms formed a grove for several blocks. Glenda turned into a driveway that wound through beds of spider lilies, ti leaves, and other tropical foliage to the porte-cochère. A smiling Hawaiian man, dressed in formal livery, opened the car doors, and they soon entered the lush, cool interior.

The Royal was a fantasy. It managed to be colorful, exotically evoking childhood fantasies, and at the same time elegant and surprisingly appropriate. She expected to find the heiress Barbara Hutton lounging in a caftan on a lobby divan. Veronica fought an inclination to ogle but instead pulled herself up straight, took a deep breath, and followed Glenda down the long hallway toward the ocean.

"Normally we'd have a drink first, but let's just go to the Monarch Room or we'll be late for our reservation. We can have a cocktail there." Glenda made her way to the maître D', who greeted her warmly and led them to a table that looked out on Waikiki Beach.

"The usual, Mrs. Preston?"

"Yes, Shige. A Manhattan for my friend, too."

Veronica smiled and nodded. She looked around the room trying to get a feel for the crowd. It was mostly couples at tables of four chattering, obviously on vacation, and an occasional romantic couple at a table for two, celebrating a special occasion.

She noticed, two tables away, two gentlemen dining with a couple. One of the men looked her way and caught her staring, so she looked away quickly.

"I just love this place, don't you?" Glenda surveyed the room. Veronica wondered if she was looking for new prey but stopped herself. Glenda needed a playmate, and she loved showing Veronica the Honolulu high life. Heaven knew there was more going on here than on Maui or, for that matter, their last stint in the Caribbean.

Glenda ordered the Waldorf salad and insisted Veronica help her with a Chateaubriand, even though she'd been eyeing the stuffed *opakapaka*. Glenda, she was discovering, was fun. She had risqué and amusing stories, it seemed, about everyone local who walked in. Before the dessert of floating islands was served, Glenda recognized the couple sitting at the table Veronica had been caught staring at earlier.

"Oh my lord. It's Barry and Jane Dilling. I've got to introduce you. He's made a virtual fortune in real estate, with his wife's money, of course. She's nice enough. A little dull for my taste."

Glenda waited until she could catch Barry Dilling's eye and gave him a little wave. He nodded in return. Veronica looked at the man who'd caught her staring earlier. He wasn't looking their way.

They were halfway through dessert when Barry stood up and walked to their table. He leaned down to give Glenda a kiss on her cheek. Glenda introduced Veronica, and as he took her hand, he asked the ladies if they would join his party for after-dinner drinks next door in the Surf Room bar.

"I'd love for you to meet Jack Wentworth and his cousin, Cyril, here from San Francisco. He's the Wentworth of Wentworth Shipping. I'm sure you've heard of him."

Glenda assured him they had and that they'd love to meet him.

When they had finished, Glenda signed the bill, announcing she kept a running account at the hotel, and they walked across the lawn to the Surf Room. The Dilling party had settled into an oceanside table and had already ordered their drinks.

"I'll have one of those minty things. You know, a crème de menthe," she said. The very thought of another drink made Veronica's stomach turn. She ordered a club soda with lots of ice.

"Gentlemen, I'd like you to meet two of our loveliest ladies," said Barry. All three men were standing. Jack and Cyril both nodded and smiled, extending their hands for a shake. Jack, she learned, loved deep-sea fishing and flying his small Cessna to meetings all over California. He was going to try to get to Kona for some local fishing before heading home. Cyril had no such interests. His family owned one of San Francisco's fanciest clothing stores, and he planned to investigate the possibility of importing a small group of island designers to the city for a summer fashion promotion.

"So what is it you do to keep the blues away?" Jack leaned toward Veronica as the others launched into a discussion of just whom Cyril should invite.

"Oh, not much," said Veronica. "I'm busy with my two children, of course, and I do volunteer work with the ladies' auxiliary. I've always wanted to try to paint, and I'm taking Saturday classes at the local school. I guess that's about it."

Jack looked at her for a long time without saying anything, making Veronica feel awkward and a little shy.

"You should work at it. Who knows, you could be very good," he smiled. Veronica noticed perfect teeth and a small dimple. "Do you ever get to San Francisco? We're having an Impressionist show at the de Young this summer. Everyone tells me it's going to be a big hit."

"Oh, believe me, I'd love to see it. My in-laws live on the peninsula, and I could stay with them, of course."

"Well, you must call me if you make it," he said, looking straight into her eyes. He reached into his jacket pocket and handed her a business card.

Veronica smiled and met his gaze. She could feel her face flush and hoped it was dark enough that no one could see. They turned back to the others.

Veronica had never been interested in politics, and local politics held even less appeal for her, but she was immediately struck by the passion it raised in Barry and the others. She'd heard the rumblings on the plantation. The management, mostly haoles and members of the Republican Party, were especially keen on tying the islands even more closely to the United States mainland. Strangely, the workers, many of them of Japanese, Portuguese, and Filipino, also wanted statehood, but for vastly different reasons. They looked to U.S. law as a way of protecting them against unjust working conditions. Hawaiians and part-Hawaiians weren't so sure but seemed divided into camps depending on their own economic stability.

"Of course, it would be marvelous," said Barry, motioning to the waiter to bring another round of drinks. "Why should we pay the same amount of taxes as everyone else in the States and have no real representation? Besides, it would be great for business. Can you just see all the money for development just waiting to come in if they were sure we were part of the Union?"

"I don't know, you might be giving up some of the uniqueness of this place. Some of its magic, if you know what I mean," said Cyril, putting out a longer than normal cigarette. Cyril exuded a hyper-refined nature that was almost feminine in its sensitivity. "I'm not saying that statehood isn't good, exactly, just that you may be getting more than you bargain for. You guys run the place now. Why rock the boat?"

Jack, who had stayed quiet on the subject, agreed with Cyril, but Barry wasn't convinced. "Listen, we run this place now, but you just watch. We already have unreasonable demands from labor. That bitch Harriet Buslog keeps making trouble with her commie friends, and then all those Nisei vets back from Europe have no intention of 'staying down on the farm,' so to speak. I think we need the good ol' USA."

Veronica just listened, unsure about where she stood. She'd heard Frank talk about some problems in the mill, but the talk had never been as open or candid as what she was hearing now in far-off Honolulu.

"Then there're all those pinkos like Jack Hall and Patsy Mink." Barry seemed unable to stop himself. "Hell, I don't know what the hell they have to complain about. This isn't the Old South. We give 'em everything they want, free medical, almost free housing. Crap!" Veronica noticed Jane Dilling had placed her hand gently on her husband's knee, calming him down immediately.

"I think it's getting past our bedtime," said Jane, rising ahead of her husband and nodding her perfectly coiffed head to those around the table. "This has been absolutely delightful. I'm so glad we ran into you and your lovely friend, Glenda. You two made this a regular party."

As they made their way to the entrance, Jack turned to Veronica. They had barely spoken two words during the evening, but she was keenly aware of him and a couple of times caught him looking at her.

"Do you get to Honolulu often?" he said.

She didn't, she replied, but she hoped to visit more and take advantage of the art classes at the Academy of Arts this summer, now that she was spending time with Glenda.

"I need the break from Maui. It's a little stifling, I'm afraid. I'm not much for country living, even though I seem to have spent much of my life there."

Jack looked at her for a long time without speaking, and Veronica began to feel uncomfortable. "That's wonderful," he said finally. "I need to be here for some negotiations. Maybe we'll run into each other again."

Veronica felt her heart start to pound and hoped her face hadn't turned red. What was she doing, feeling this disoriented over a man she hardly knew? She thought of his card in her evening bag.

"That would be nice," she said, walking faster to catch up with Glenda and trying to appear calm. They all said their goodbyes as the cars were delivered to the entrance.

"My, my," said Glenda when they were settled in her little MG and headed down Kalakaua Avenue. "I couldn't help but notice you and Jack Wentworth. Careful, Veronica. He's got every eligible woman in San Francisco and beyond after him, and need I mention that you already have your hands full? Fun is fun. I can't believe I'm saying this, but don't lose your head, darling."

Veronica looked at her and shrugged. "Oh, silly. That was absolutely nothing." She turned to watch the road in front of them, but there was a lump in her throat. They were quiet the rest of the way home.

The next morning, Veronica found Glenda already doing laps in her pool. The day was one of those perfect ones that comes just as the seasons are about to change, when the air is still cool and the trade winds gentle. Glenda's maid brought freshly squeezed orange juice, coffee, and English muffins to a table under the striped cabana and Veronica settled into a chaise to watch Glenda. She swam effortlessly. Veronica sat wishing she were as graceful in the water. Glenda was long, tall, and permanently tanned. Like so many haole women who grew up on the islands, she looked as if she had been raised in a bathing suit. It was an attitude of being completely comfortable with your body.

The two spent the rest of the day laughing and trading stories. She found she liked Glenda tremendously. For all her bluster, Glenda was a kind and generous person. Veronica suspected she also was very lonely. It was past noon before they moved from the poolside, and Glenda had gotten up just once to take a call from Jane Dilling to tell her what a grand time they'd had and how much they'd enjoyed meeting Veronica.

"We'll have to do this again," Glenda said as Veronica hurried to pack her things for her late afternoon flight. "You have a very nice way, Veronica. You're easy to be with. I find I talk and talk and then realize you've said next to nothing about yourself. Naughty girl, I'm going to have to get you to open up, too."

Glenda drove Veronica to the interisland terminal and gave her a hug at the gate. Jack Wentworth had not been mentioned all day, but Veronica found herself thinking about him as she settled into her seat. He was a handsome enough man, but not in the conventional way. In fact, he was quite ordinary until he spoke. His voice commanded you to listen, and when you answered, he looked at you directly with almost alarming candor. It was this ability to listen that made him so attractive. Not to mention the fact that he had gobs of money.

As the plane approached Maui, Veronica saw out her window the green cane fields in the central valley and up the slopes of the West Maui mountains laid out before her. Pineapple crops crawled up Haleakala to the neat rows of wooden camp houses that made up Hali'imaile. Every so often more houses appeared surrounded by the patterned fields. It looked so peaceful and orderly. So unlike what she was now feeling.

She wondered at her own reaction to Jack. Veronica, who was always so cool and in charge when it came to the men in her life, had been profoundly affected by this man. She was the one who chose, never waiting to be chosen. Money and authority had always been alluring, as they were for so many women. But she had been drawn to Jack in a new and different way, to the easy way he laughed and commanded attention from everyone, including Barry Dilling, who was well known for his pomposity. Her attraction to him had been visceral. It was in the way his hair hit his collar and his hands held a glass. She'd found herself staring at his mouth as he spoke. There was an ease with which Jack Wentworth approached the world, and Veronica felt safe in his presence. It had taken only an hour to disturb the sense of comfort she had just begun to feel on Maui.

SHE ARRIVED HOME TO FIND FRANK happy from his fishing trip and the children excited to see them both. Chip had spent the weekend learning the basics of woodworking in Manuel Cravalho's backyard workshop, and Heidi had baked Meyer lemon bars with Hattie. The moment Veronica arrived home, Heidi ran to her mother, her words tumbling out with enthusiasm. The girl's cheeks were flushed and her hair almost white blonde. *She must have spent some time on the beach, too,* Veronica thought.

Chip was more reserved but obviously proud of the wooden box Manuel had helped him make. He ran his fingers along the edges of the box made of mango wood, explaining how difficult it had been to make the top fit perfectly. He was happier and more animated than he'd been in a long time.

Although they were all tired, an easy contentment settled among them over dinner that night. They were a family again.

As the school year wound down, Veronica threw herself into planning an afternoon tea to help raise funds for school supplies for camp children, to be used when public school reopened in the fall. The mothers of Kaunoa students, aware of their own children's distinct advantages, felt it necessary to help wherever they could.

Veronica found herself heading the refreshment committee. She planned to ask Hattie to make her coconut and peach turnovers, already famous among the ladies. She asked the mothers of two of Heidi's classmates to help her arrange it all. It wasn't exactly stimulating, but it gave Veronica something to occupy her time. She forced herself not to think about Jack Wentworth and the disturbing way he'd made her feel.

Glenda called once a week to see how Veronica was adjusting and seemed happy herself. She'd had a few dates with a new man she'd met through friends at the Outrigger and the two now were fully involved. Maybe you'll get down this summer, she said. Bring the children. There're some great classes for kids at Punahou and the Academy.

Veronica promised she'd think about it.

She became more interested in the dinner table talks about what was happening in the camps with the labor movement. Frank and the other plantation managers were clearly concerned. There had been flare-ups before. Filipino workers had risen up on Kauai before Pearl Harbor. There'd been shots fired and men killed. Some plantation supervisors remembered the ILWU union strike of 1949 when longshoremen on the docks of Honolulu demanded the same wages and working conditions as their mainland counterparts. It had nearly shut down the sugar and pineapple industries. While it didn't affect Frank's work in the laboratory directly, he was concerned. His own inclinations were more liberal than most of his fellow managers. He could see changes were necessary.

Veronica again found herself wondering about Jack. His shipping company did business in the islands. Had he been involved? She wanted him to be a good guy, one who treated people fairly, but she wasn't sure where he stood.

Planning the fundraiser took up more of her time than she'd anticipated. *What is it about women's organizations?* she thought *Why do they have to have so many meetings?* It seemed to Veronica that so much of it was busywork designed just to take up time. It irritated her, but she had joined out of a desire to keep busy.

On the morning of the tea, as Frank was getting ready for work, he mentioned that Barry Dilling had been talking to Harold Balding about another matter—the two were second cousins on their mother's sides—and Barry had mentioned to Harold how taken he, Jane, Jack, and Cyril had been with Veronica.

"You didn't tell me you'd met Jack Wentworth," said Frank, trying to adjust a tie on the collar of his short-sleeved white shirt.

"Hmm, yeah. I did. He seemed nice enough," Veronica said as she emerged from the shower. Hearing Frank say Jack's name startled her. She was unprepared with an answer and wondered why it bothered her at all.

"Apparently, Barry and Jane had the idea he would definitely have liked to see much more of you." Frank splashed aftershave on his freshly shaven face and turned to her, his forehead knitted.

"Oh, for God's sake, Frank! What are you saying? You aren't jealous, are you?" Veronica laughed, trying to sound casual. "Come on, sweetie, I met him at dinner. He was nice, end of story." Veronica pretended a pout and planted a long, slow kiss on Frank's lips. It aroused him and he dropped the subject. She was relieved.

"Off you go." She patted his behind and sent him on his way.

WITH SUMMER FAST APPROACHING, THE ELECTION season began to heat up. Until recently, candidates had either been put up by the Big Five companies on the Republican ticket or by independent business men and women who could belong to both parties. Veronica found politics on the islands both fascinating and hilarious. Rallies on Maui mostly were held in movie theaters owned by one of the men running for office. Louie Paschoal was a rotund and imposing man of Portuguese descent. Born on the sugar plantation in Wailuku, he'd worked and saved his money to start a movie theater. He had found an empty building in Waikapu that was no more than a barn and lacked half a roof. Undaunted, Paschoal leased the building and installed a movie screen and projector and had a local Japanese carpenter build benches, which he lined up to face the screen.

Movies ran every night of the week—Filipino films on Monday, Japanese on Tuesday and Wednesday. He saved the Hollywood movies for the rest of the week. The theaters were so popular that in a couple of years he opened two more movie houses, this time with the encouragement of plantation managers who were only too happy to keep workers happy and occupied; the alternatives had been gambling, prostitution, and cock fighting. Before long, every town on the island had a Paschoal theater.

The candidates began the rallies by driving through the plantation camps on the backs of pickups and flatbed trucks fitted with public address systems. Often, trios of Hawaiian musicians riding along on the trucks accompanied the candidates to the theater, where the speeches and entertainment really began. Candidates appeared on stage wearing their best suits and covered with so many leis they often couldn't see where they were going and were forced to remove a few. The whole spectacle delighted and amused Veronica, and she begged Frank to take her. He finally relented and agreed to go once or twice. But she found a kindred spirit in Hattie. On rally nights, she and Hattie jumped into Veronica's two-toned Chevrolet coupe and headed out. Hattie always packed a thermos of coffee as well as ham sandwiches smeared with lots of mayonnaise and lettuce. To her surprise, Veronica realized her comfort with Hattie stemmed from the fact that Hattie reminded her of her own mother, Eula.

The night the rally was held in Paia, Frank stayed at home with the children and Hattie packed their picnic supper. They quickly settled themselves into their seats in the loge section usually reserved for haoles. (Amazingly, on Hawaiian plantations, the Portuguese were not considered haoles—they were in a category all their own.) The hula dancers' supporting candidate Ransom Sakai had just taken the stage when the woman from the box office tapped Veronica on the shoulder to tell her she had an urgent phone call. It was Frank.

"Veronica, are you with Hattie?" his voice sounded tense.

She said that she was.

"There's been an accident at the mill. It's Manuel. He got his arm caught in one of the rollers, and they've taken him to the Puunene Hospital. I think he may lose it. Do you think you can drive Hattie there?"

Veronica tried to compose herself before returning to her seat to get Hattie. "We have to go," was all she said until she and Hattie got outside and were walking to the car. She explained the situation as she drove them down the mountain to lower Paia, with its wooden storefronts looking like something out of a movie western, past the Maui Country Club, now dark, at Spreckelsville. As Veronica turned off the Hana Highway onto a poorly lit, two-lane road leading through the cane fields to the hospital, she revved the engine. Hattie sat up straight, quiet, with her eyes focused on the road. She hardly seemed to breathe.

Manuel lost his left arm that night. Hattie, clearly upset, took a week off until he was discharged from the hospital. He'd never been a man who talked much. With Hattie, he'd never needed to. The two of them were so in sync it was as if she automatically knew what he was thinking. They had a way of bickering constantly, yet there was no doubt they adored each other. She stayed home with him for another week but then insisted on coming back to work. Their oldest daughter would come to stay with Manuel during the day.

"He making me nuts. 'Go get dis, go get dat.' Aiye. Wat I going do? More bettah I come work." Hattie was on her hands and knees scrubbing the linoleum floor in the kitchen.

Veronica was not going to argue with Hattie. The two of them worked on refreshments for the fundraiser, which turned out to make more money for school supplies than anyone had expected. Veronica was pleased. She asked Frank for a little extra allowance to give Hattie as a bonus. She knew Hattie was struggling now with extra expenses and Manuel on sick leave.

Veronica had gotten into a nice routine over the last month, and she and Frank had settled into contentedness. Then Glenda called from Honolulu. She hadn't heard from Veronica and wanted her to come with the children and stay the summer.

"Get them stimulated. Put them in art classes at the Honolulu Academy of Arts and get them riding lessons at Kapiolani Park. There's so much happening here this summer. You owe it to them, Veronica. Besides that, I could use the company. My new love is off to Europe this summer with his mother. Can you imagine that? With his *mother*."

Hearing Glenda on the phone reminded her of her attraction to Jack. She wondered if he was in town but decided not to ask. Frank urged her to go. She agreed finally and called the numbers Glenda had given her in order to enroll the children in classes. Within a week, they were all on the plane on their way to "town," as everyone called Honolulu.

Glenda had made her guest cottage ready for the family, filling the refrigerator with snacks, a bottle of vodka and tonic water for Veronica, and papaya and English muffins for breakfast. There were board games—Monopoly and Chinese checkers, a cribbage board, a deck of cards, puzzles. After dropping Heidi and Chip off at the Academy each morning, Veronica joined Glenda for laps in her pool. Within a week, Veronica's hair had bleached out and her skin was a light golden tan. What's more, she felt wonderful. Glenda's maid, Fumiko, a plain Japanese woman of indeterminate age, stayed with the children when Glenda and Veronica wanted a night out, which was often.

Whenever Glenda had friends in for cocktails, Fumiko got dressed up in a silk kimono with a stiff obi and served drinks and *pupu* on lacquer trays. Glenda's parties were always fun with a casual elegance that was freer, wilder than those on the plantation. The conversation was lively and dealt with topics that would never have been discussed on Maui, where mostly people talked shop.

Glenda had a charming way of letting guests know it was time to leave. She would sit at the piano and play softly as Fumiko and her helpers passed steaming cups of soup, both as a hint that it was time to go and an attempt to sober some of them up. They always left; they wanted to be invited back.

VERONICA AND THE CHILDREN SETTLED INTO their own routine by their second week. They woke early, and while Veronica took a morning swim in Glenda's Olympic-sized, saltwater pool, Heidi and Chip ran to the beach to find Uncle Kino. Veronica wasn't sure of the relationship Uncle Kino had to Glenda's family, but he clearly had the run of the place, coming and going as he wished, placing his fishnets according to some mysterious cycle of the moon. Uncle

Kino was a pure-blooded Hawaiian, his skin darkened by the sun and the whites of his eyes yellowed by sun and water exposure. He was missing at least four front teeth, but it never stopped his bright smile whenever he saw the children. Chip was learning to "throw net," as Uncle Kino put it, and Heidi just liked tagging along to hear his stories of magic and myths.

Glenda often joined Veronica at the pool after her second cup of coffee. Today, she seemed in especially high spirits. Glenda's new love had returned to his wife, and she'd been moping around the house for the last few days. But today she was in better spirits.

"Hooray, some much-needed diversion, darling!"

Glenda, barefoot and wearing a long, animal-printed caftan, dropped unceremoniously into a lounge chair beside Veronica. She had just gotten off the phone with Jane Dilling, who had called to invite them both to spend the weekend at the Dillings' house in Mokuleia.

"Thank God, a distraction from my misery. I know, I know, I'm old enough to know better," she said, taking a sip of coffee. "Don't worry about the kids, they'll be fine here with Fumiko and Uncle Kino. You're going to love this place, Val. Everyone's dying to get the nod. There's always someone new, the food's great, and the drinks never stop. Believe me, it's gin fizzes for breakfast, bloody marys for lunch, and martinis at dinner. It'll give you a chance to see the North Shore, too."

Veronica had been enjoying her time alone with the kids, but she knew Glenda needed this more than she did. Her calls from Frank had been further and further apart, but rather than being concerned, she felt relieved. It struck her how rarely she thought of life on Maui.

On Friday after lunch, they headed for Mokuleia in Glenda's MG. Fumiko had squeezed fresh orange juice for screwdrivers, which they consumed on the road. Past Kalihi the two-lane highway wound, past the Damons' property at Salt Lake. Sam Damon's house, a magnificent example of prewar contemporary architecture, sat at the top of a bluff overlooking Pearl Harbor. A friend of Glenda's lived in one of the smaller Damon houses on the property below at Moanalua. It was an old wooden structure with rococo trim that had once been visited by Hawaiian royalty, Glenda pointed out as they flew past the gardens.

By the time they reached Waipahu, cane fields lined both sides of the road. She was struck by the similarity to Maui. All the sugar companies had followed the same general layout when planning their plantation towns.

When they reached Mokuleia, it was midafternoon and Veronica was sleepy from the ride and the drinks. She clearly wasn't used to Glenda's lifestyle, especially all the alcohol. They drove past the gate and up a long driveway to a low structure not visible from the road. A houseboy dressed in white showed them into the cool, dark interior and went to get Jane Dilling.

"I say, darling, it'll be fun to see who Jane's put together this time."

The main room was large with a stone fireplace on one end. Books lined two walls and card tables were pulled up near the windows on one side. In front of the fireplace were two well-worn, comfortable-looking sofas and a coffee table of monkeypod wood. The legs had been intricately carved and polished. The entire room was pulled together with an enormous woven *lauhala* floor mat.

Jane Dilling came to greet them wearing a pair of denim jeans, loafers, and a simple white blouse. Two golden Labradors who clearly had the run of the house tagged along at her side.

"It's so nice to see you two. I've been out here all week with the horses and I'm dying for company. Barry's gone down to the airstrip to pick up Jack. You two remember him, don't you? He's here for some negotiations with the stevedores, and I suspect he could use the break too. The Singletons and the Wildings came this morning, and I've put them in the Plumeria cottage. I thought you girls would like the privacy of the Hibiscus."

Glenda shot her a look, but Veronica kept her gaze upon Jane. Warmth shot through her body and she struggled, hoping it had not yet reached her face and turned it beet red.

"Shige will show you the way to Hibiscus cottage, but Glenda, I think you remember it, don't you, dear?"

Shige, now in middle age, had worked for the Dillings since he was out of high school. He picked up their weekend cases, and they all left for the guesthouse, taking a path lined with naupaka, a hardy hedge that loved the salt and sea air. The cottage had two bedrooms, each of which opened onto a shared veranda with koa wood rockers. Veronica spotted another cottage across the lawn that she assumed was Plumeria.

"Cocktails at six in the main house," said Shige. "Mrs. Dilling expects everyone to be on time. She does have one rule: no drinking in the rooms."

Veronica looked quizzically at Glenda. What a puzzle these people were. They drank like fish most of the time, but there was still this puritanical sense of propriety underlying it all.

"Well, I'm putting my feet up. I'm bushed," said Glenda, dropping heavily onto her bed covered with a light cotton spread.

"I think I'll look around. This place is amazing. It's so casual and unassuming, so why do I think it reeks of privilege?"

"Because it's private, darling—private, exclusive, and all theirs. Haven't you noticed yet? What we have may not be as flashy as mainland money, but we have access, keys to gates to special places." Glenda turned away and within seconds was snoring gently.

Instead of walking, Veronica stepped outside, sat in one of the rockers, putting her bare feet on the railing, and closed her eyes. The summer break had relaxed her. She had hardly thought of Frank the entire time, and when he called, which was rarely, he talked to the children most of the time.

She looked back at the main house and saw a man coming down the naupaka pathway toward the cottage. He wore a cotton shirt tucked into casual slacks, and a hat shielded his face from the late afternoon sun. Veronica felt her stomach clench. *Oh no,* she thought. *Oh no.*

Jack Wentworth saw her, hesitated, then proceeded toward the cottage.

"Nice to see you again, Mrs. Caldwell," he nodded, removing his hat. He seemed more formal than he had before, causing Veronica to wonder whether he felt the same pull between them that she did. He looked tired and his tan had faded.

"And the same to you, Mr. Wentworth. I hear you've been here meeting with stevedores. I hope your negotiations are going well."

"Well enough," he said, turning to look out across the lawn. "I see we'll be right next to each other. Are you here with Glenda?"

"Yes, she's napping."

He nodded politely. "Why don't I knock before we go for drinks and dinner? We can all walk over together."

"That would be lovely. Glenda will be happy to see you."

He looked at Veronica, nodded again, and with a slight smile opened the creaky screen door to his room.

ON SATURDAY MORNING, VERONICA WOKE TO the sound of chickens making a racket outside the cottage window. She lay in bed staring at the ceiling and wondered if she'd just imagined the night before. Jack had kept his distance throughout the cocktail hour and had been seated next to Jane Dilling at dinner. She had wondered if he was purposely avoiding catching her eye. Veronica had thought she would steer clear of him during the evening, but it seemed he was doing the same to her. His reversal of interest irritated her.

There was a soft knock at the cottage door and a woman of about thirty entered with a tray of coffee, cups, and fresh pineapple juice. She left them on the table by the door, smiled and nodded at Veronica, and left as quietly as she'd appeared.

Glenda had really tied one on the night before, and Veronica didn't expect her to be up for hours. Barry and Jane Dilling had strict rules about appearing for the cocktail hour, but the remainder of the guests' day was up to them. A table was set for breakfast, and guests could help themselves whenever they wanted. Lunch was always simple—a salad, sandwich fixings, and sometimes a cold soup. Shige's wife, Noriko, made legendary chocolate chip cookies and often sent tins of them home with guests she especially liked. Veronica realized it was Noriko who had brought their tray of coffee.

After breakfast, she went back to check on Glenda, who was still fast asleep, her eyes covered with a satin sleep mask and the covers pulled up under her chin. *She looks like a child*, thought Veronica. She put on her swim suit, wrapped herself in a pareu, and stuck an old lauhala hat she'd found in the closet on her head and walked to the beach.

The tide was low, exposing parts of the coral reef. Veronica found a spot on the warm sand and lathered herself with Monoi coconut oil. For a while, she watched a swimmer doing laps parallel to the shore. But soon she settled down on her back and enjoyed the warmth of the morning sun on her face and body.

The sun and sound of the waves lapping calmly on the shore almost lulled her to sleep. She couldn't remember ever being this relaxed and cared for. If she didn't have to, she'd never leave this place.

Veronica was startled back to reality by drops of cold water on her bare torso. She opened her eyes. Standing over her was a man, and for a moment she felt only alarm.

"I didn't mean to frighten you," said Jack, dripping salt water and smiling at her.

She sat up. "So it was you out there."

"I don't think anyone else is up yet." Jack dropped to the sand next to her. "It's a nice time of day, isn't it?"

"I've always loved mornings. They're so fresh and new. So full of possibilities."

Jack smiled and nodded. "Have you ever been on a glider?"

"A what?"

"You know, like a small airplane, only without an engine. You just glide. It's the closest thing to being a bird. I know a guy who's got one out at the airfield. He's been asking me to come out and I never do. Why don't you come with me?"

"Okay. It sounds like fun." She surprised herself by answering so quickly.

They walked back to the cottage, Veronica slightly behind Jack, trying to avoid stepping on sharp cones from the ironwood trees that lined the sand. She slipped into the cottage quietly so as not to wake Glenda, who had thrown off her sheets and was bare-assed. Veronica pulled on a pair of white shorts and an oversized T-shirt with a pair of sandals. Jack met her on the lanai wearing a faded golf shirt and shorts.

"Let's take my car," he said.

They drove the short distance to the Mokuleia airstrip. Jack had apparently called his friend from his room because the man was waiting near what looked like a small airplane but clearly wasn't. He made the introductions and they climbed into the glider. Jack went first and helped Veronica in, settling her right in front of him. They were so close she was aware of his breath on the back of her neck and his arms almost around her, holding the sides of the glider.

"Relax, I won't bite," he said.

*Easy for him*, she thought as the glider started down the runway. Within seconds they were in the air. All she could think about was how quiet it was as the glider soared along the coast, with its blue water, coral reefs, and sand below. It made a slow turn inland over neat rows of pineapple, and she could make out the Dillings' compound. What would they all think if they could see her . . . could see *them*? Veronica felt herself relax as the wind blew her hair and she felt the warmth of Jack behind her.

GLENDA WAS QUIET ON THE RIDE back into Honolulu the next afternoon. That worked just fine for Veronica. Her head was filled with the weekend and Jack. He continued to seek her out at dinner Saturday night and at breakfast the next morning. She was sure Barry and Jane had noticed, and she wondered if either of them would say something, but so far they hadn't. The chemistry between Veronica and Jack had been impossible to deny.

They reached Diamond Head and Glenda broke her silence.

"Need to talk?"

Veronica nodded. "But not right now, okay?"

"Sure, honey. Tomorrow."

The next morning, Veronica found Glenda having coffee at the pool. She'd already done her laps and was reading the newspaper. She looked up as Veronica approached.

"Coffee?"

"Hmmm."

"Did you sleep well?"

Veronica nodded and plopped herself into a lounge chair. "Another day in paradise!" They chatted about the headlines. Harry Bridges, the longshoremen's union negotiator was in town and all of Bishop Street was girding for a fight. The Big Five companies who controlled Hawaii had made the rules for a long time, and they weren't about to give up control to some lowlife troublemaker like Bridges.

"Shall we talk about what's going on with you, Veronica?"

"Don't be angry with me, Glenda. I didn't plan for this to happen, but I can't stop myself. "

"I guess that's sort of obvious." Glenda didn't seem very upset, just concerned.

"Before I met Jack, I'd sort of resigned myself to plantation life, to the sameness of the days and country living. I'll admit I wasn't always content, but I was getting better. Now I'm beginning to think I've been half dead. The crazy thing is I hardly know him. I just know I like how I feel when I'm with him."

Glenda didn't reply right away but looked out beyond the pool at the ocean.

"Oh, the gossips will have a field day with this one," she said finally. "Listen, Veronica, I love having you and the kids here. You're such damn good company. What's more, I understand. You're not the first plantation wife to fly the coop, and you won't be the last. Promise me you'll take it slow with Jack. He's got a lot going on now. Get to know him better before you decide to throw everything in the air and bolt."

"I will. But I need to keep seeing him, Glenda. How else will I know if what I feel is mutual? I think it is for him too, but it's too soon."

"Sure, but see him here, and make sure there's a place for your children in his life before you go doing anything radical."

Veronica gave Glenda a hug. "You're a rare creature, my friend."

Glenda smiled and gave her a shrug. She got up and headed for the house to change her clothes. She was modeling for Alfred Shaheen at the Royal Hawaiian at lunch and needed to get ready.

Veronica was relieved. Jack wanted to see more of her, and she desperately wanted to be with him. She'd never felt so passionate about a man and at the same time so safe. The combination intoxicated her and she couldn't stop it.

Just then, Fumiko appeared with more coffee, popovers, and poha jam. Chip and Heidi had already gone to the beach with Uncle Kino, leaving Veronica alone for the rest of the morning.

"I'm so sorry, Miz Caldwell. Mr. Wentworth called earlier and I thought you was still in bed. He want you call him at his office."

A YEAR LATER, GLENDA PRESTON HAD just finished her morning swim when Fumiko brought a tray of coffee and *The Honolulu Advertiser* to her poolside. Glenda glanced at the headlines: "Mink is Pink!" It was another story about Patsy Mink, the Democratic legislator and labor leader who was now accused of having Communist ties. *Will those old Bishop Street fogies ever stop?* thought Glenda. *Have they no shame?*

She opened the paper to the society pages in case there had been any important parties she hadn't been invited to, but on page two, in Stella Wilcox's column, an item jumped out at her.

*Mr. John "Jack" Wentworth of San Francisco and Mrs. Veronica Caldwell, formerly of Hawaii, were married earlier this month in an intimate ceremony at the Carmel ranch of Mr. Wentworth's longtime friend, Cyril Fairfield. Mr. Wentworth is the principle owner of Wentworth Shipping, Inc., which was founded by his father, Hugh Wentworth. Mrs. Caldwell wore a cream lace sheath with satin pumps and was attended by her children, Frank, Jr., and Heidi Caldwell. The family will reside at Mr. Wentworth's Pacific Heights home.*

Glenda folded the paper and rang the little bell she kept beside her while at the pool. "Fumiko! Fumiko! Bring me a screwdriver! Not the tool either; I want a drink!"

Fumiko appeared in a few minutes with a tall glass filled with orange juice and vodka on ice.

"Well, Veronica darling, you got what you really wanted, didn't you?" Glenda said, shaking her head.

# EMMA

Emma Akau awoke one Saturday in the summer of 1949 and knew beyond a doubt her life would never be the same. It was too early for the phone to start ringing, so she lay motionless under the soft bedcovers on which her mother, Helen, had stitched pale flowers the year she'd married Harold. Emma wasn't ready to talk to anyone, even though she knew that she would have to eventually.

Nobody in her family had been happy when Emma announced she was going to marry Harold. Just Emma. Her mother had thought him too common and not quite aspirational enough. But Emma had loved everything about Harold—his too-long face, craggy even though he was only twenty-two; his long, lanky frame, all angles, the kind that never would put on extra pounds as the years passed. Those years would never pass now. Harold was dead, lying cold in the refrigerator at Norman's Mortuary on Lower Main Street. Emma shivered and pulled the covers up closer. She felt too tired to cry.

The night before, a doctor came into the corridor of the hospital in Wailuku, where Emma had set up her makeshift camp with blankets, a bento box with food, and a change of clothes. She wasn't leaving Harold. The hospital had never been intended as a hospital. It had opened during World War II, when the U.S. military had taken over the existing high school. But it had remained after the war, and now beds sometimes lined the hallways, and they were always short of doctors and staff.

It had all come so suddenly, Emma thought. She had never expected Harold to be so sick. He was barely thirty-two. Men that young had died all the time during the war, but not now. Certainly not Harold. They said his heart had given out during the surgery to remove his infected kidney.

Emma lay quietly in bed watching the lace curtains move with every slight breeze and began to cry. Quietly the warm tears trickled down her brown face onto the pillowcase. Soon her chest heaved and she was sobbing uncontrollably.

"Harold, Harold." She remembered that their daughter, Deanie, was down the street at her grandmother's house, and Emma was alone. Her mother had kept Deanie for the night, knowing she needed to sleep and be alone.

Years ago, when Emma and Harold had told her mother about the engagement, Helen had just stared straight ahead, her jaw tightening and her lips pressing more closely together. Emma suspected Helen had wanted her to aim higher; to elevate her station in society. Her mother never said much. So perhaps she'd never had high hopes for her anyway. Emma thought herself the least attractive of Helen's four daughters.

Emma knew her mother had always intended for her girls to marry well. She had drummed it into their heads from the time they were old enough to understand. Marrying the right man with a good education and job was the key to their futures, she had told them. Helen had married the right man, but he too had become sick and died early in their marriage, leaving her with the girls to raise on a teacher's small salary. With that and a small inheritance from her family, she managed to raise her spirited, opinionated girls. By marrying properly, they could perhaps achieve something even better for themselves.

Emma thought about her sisters. Alma had that misty, wispy way of floating through life. There was a spunkiness, too. It made her an enigma, one that everyone, men and women both, found compelling.

Iwalani was the real stunner. Her skin was so fair and her eyes so blue, she was often mistaken for a haole. Emma remembered when they had been young and Helen would pile the girls into their old Ford to take them to see their grandparents in Paia. The girls' grandfather, an Englishman, had operated the plantation cane train, and their grandmother was native Hawaiian. They would all sit primly in the parlor while their grandmother served them her famous prune cake with fresh guava juice. Their grandfather had always given the girls coins as treats when they left. Everyone would get dimes. But on the ride home, Iwalani would open her palm. She alone would have been given a quarter.

Iwalani would smile slyly. "He loves me more," she'd say. "Look."

Emma's youngest sister, Clare, was two years behind her, but Clare had developed into a beauty much earlier. She was small and curvy, with a temper and personality that at once challenged and flirted with everyone. Sometimes dealing with Clare was like mistakenly petting a tiger cub because it was cute.

Emma knew she wasn't pretty. Her hair was kinky and her eyes just a bit too large. They made her look pop-eyed when she got excited. "Bug eyes," her sisters had called her. Her skin was darker than that of anyone else in the family, although no one spoke openly about it or teased her. She was plain and homely in this family of beauties.

To make matters worse, she liked to read all the time. She devoured books, magazines, anything she could get her hands on. After school, she had been happiest walking to the Wailuku Public Library to do her homework. She'd get lost in the stacks, reading for hours about the universe, politics in Argentina, the rice harvest in South China. Emma had been curious about everything. Her sisters had teased her, said she was always away somewhere in a dream world. But anyone who paid enough attention to her favorite subjects and her quirky interests could expect a radiant smile along with hours of deep, complex conversation. Emma had another thing going for her: she was tall and slim. No one looked better than she did in a pair of shorts. Emma had known immediately after meeting Harold that they matched up perfectly.

The church bells started to ring at St. Anthony's. It was just six o'clock. Emma pulled the covers tighter, trying not to move, and listened to her own breathing. She wanted to hold Harold and her love for him close. She didn't want to talk to anyone, answer questions, or listen to their condolences. She wanted to be with Harold, if only in her mind, alone in this room.

There had always been something quiet about him. He had never needed to be the center of attention, but he had made Emma the center of his life. Every day he had gotten up early and headed down to the sugar mill where he had worked as a mechanic on the big crushers that extracted the syrup from the cane. When Emma would wake, the coffee would be made and Deanie would be content in her crib, having already been fed. Harold could fix anything. He took his father's old model T with the crank starter and made it hum. He fixed fans, lawnmowers, clocks, anything that was broken. But he couldn't fix this. He couldn't fix what was going on inside her right this minute.

Emma thought back two years, to when she and Harold had been expecting their second child. Deanie was still two years old then, a chubby girl who sucked her thumb and was attached to her flannel blanket. Emma had become pregnant again and they were all happy. She'd had no problem during the pregnancy, except that she'd wanted to sleep all the time. But she had never gotten sick and rarely had the mood swings common among her friends and sisters. Her first pregnancy had gone without a problem.

On the day her water broke, she had been baking the chocolate chip cookies Harold and Deanie loved. He raced home from the mill to take her to the hospital.

The same hospital he lay in last night.

The delivery was difficult, and the nurses became more and more concerned when the doctor didn't show up. He had been at a party at a beach house in Makena. They tried to keep Emma as comfortable as they could, even though they knew he would arrive more than a little drunk.

They made an effort to comfort Emma and reassure Harold, but the hours dragged on and still no doctor. When he finally came, everyone was relieved. He'd obviously tried to sober up by washing his face and drinking coffee, but the stale smell of alcohol still clung to him.

Emma's baby came finally. She was a little girl, seven pounds three ounces. But she was already dead. Emma's labor had been too long and the umbilical cord wrapped around the baby's neck had strangled her.

Emma felt numb. But Harold was there comforting and reassuring her. She wondered if he was angry, but she couldn't tell. Not yet. They would have another, she thought. She could bear anything with him close to her.

Now he wasn't. He never would be again.

Emma turned in bed and buried her face in the pillow. It hurt too much. It took a while for her to realize it, but today was her birthday. She was twenty-eight years old.

# THE ANCESTOR

It drizzled the morning Lily flew into Hilo airport. *It's always drizzling in Hilo*, she thought, collecting her handbag bulging with media releases and the camera from under the seat in front of her. She was in Hilo on assignment from a Honolulu newspaper.

Lily loved the freedom of working out of town as much as she hated being stuck in the newsroom doing rewrites. By noon, the skies had cleared and she was finished with her interviews. But there were still hours to kill until her late afternoon flight home.

Lily's granny, Helen Kamanu, had been born and raised in Hilo, and much of her family still lived here. Lily's mother, Clare, and her aunts had spent each summer growing up in the 1930s with their cousins in the sleepy seaside town. But Lily knew almost no one well enough to pick up the phone and make a call, even for a casual cup of coffee. The thought of it made her intensely shy, something she was rarely accused of being.

Instead, she poked into the stores lining Hilo Bay, picking up a cotton kimono in Dragon Mama and stopping for a salad at Café Pesto. But there were still a couple of hours until her flight.

"What is there to do other than shop and eat in this town?" she said good-naturedly to her waitress, not wanting to insult.

"Not much," the woman, who had once been pretty but now had the rumpled, careless look of an aging hippie, smiled back. "Have you been up to the museum yet, or over to Reed's Island?"

"Not in years," said Lily, "but that gives me an idea. Thanks." She collected her shopping bags and purse and headed for her rental car. She would use the time to see what she could discover about Ah Chan.

Ever since Lily had heard about her Granny Kamanu's Chinese grandfather, back when she was still in high school, Ah Chan had fascinated her. She'd once made a half-hearted attempt at writing a paper on him while at Kamehameha School. But it had been amateurish, filled with drama. From time to time, she would come across something about early Chinese settlers to the islands and she'd copy and file it, meaning to pick it back up again when she had time.

What had always intrigued Lily was that nothing about her own appearance seemed to connect her to this Chinese man. The marriages of relatives that took place during the years between them—to Hawaiians, the French, the Swedish, the Irish—had wiped every Chinese physical characteristic from her face. Lily's hair was dark with hints of auburn in the sunlight; her skin freckled when she spent too much time outdoors. And her body was, to put it bluntly, sturdy, or "big-boned," as her mother always said in a vaguely critical tone.

She wondered whether his blood really ran in her veins. Had he been like her in any way? She, too, was determined. She, too, loved the excitement of stepping foot in a new and strange place. She loved traveling in Asia with its strong smells, its chaos and frenetic energy. But she never kidded herself that she belonged to it. She was too American, too bold and out of place. Lily felt a better understanding of Ah Chan would supply a key, helping her to understand herself. It had become a selfish yet urgent need in recent years.

Lily thought back to when she'd first heard of him. A woman from the University of Hawaii had come to visit Granny Kamanu on a day when Lily, then 15, had dropped in to borrow old towels to take to the beach. The woman sat at Granny's chrome kitchen table with the bright yellow Formica top and placed a small tape recorder in front of her. Granny looked uncomfortable, and Lily sensed her relief when Lily decided to hang around awhile to listen.

"What are your first memories of your grandfather?" the woman asked as Granny fidgeted, crossing her legs first one way and then another. She was dressed in one of the housedresses with tiny flowers she had always worn in the 1950s. Her feet were bare except for a pair of homemade lauhala slippers she had purchased from the Japanese ladies at the Hongwanji church's annual sale and only wore inside the house.

Granny was small and delicate with pale-coffee skin and wiry, gray hair that she brushed out each morning into a voluminous cloud before twisting and knotting it into a neat chignon at the nape of her neck. Lily and her cousins had watched this process in awe on many mornings after an overnight stay, amazed that something so big and wild could become so small and tidy.

Granny had been lovely as a young woman. Lily's mother had once told her the upright player piano in the corner of Granny's living room, the one no one ever played, had been given to her when she'd won a beauty contest in Hilo. Granny was quiet, modest, and very stubborn—qualities that served her well in the years after her husband died, leaving her with five children to raise on her teaching salary.

Ah Chan was Granny's grandfather. He'd come from China—probably from Quandong province, they had guessed because of his knowledge of growing sugar cane—sometime in the early 1840s. It was thought he'd worked for years aboard foreign vessels, going in and out of the port of Canton, but it was clear he was on the Big Island of Hawaii near Kawaihae by 1842.

He and a small group of Chinese sugar masters, all adventurers with obscure pasts, had set up a series of primitive mills to produce the sweet brown cakes of sugar they sold to the local population and the crews of ships that put into Kawaihae for provisions. The researcher was trying to find out more about these early Chinese settlers. Obviously an independent group, they had been quickly assimilated into the Hawaiian population, becoming entrepreneurs and marrying island women. They would never experience the struggles and indignities of the Chinese who came later to work Hawaii's fields. They worked as hard, but they were always their own men, never indentured.

"Do you have any photographs of him?" the researcher inquired, smiling at Granny, trying to get her to relax and open up.

Granny just shook her head. She was a tough interview; even Lily realized it. Granny had become used to not giving up information. She didn't know how to open up even when she wanted to, especially about the past and certainly not to this haole woman.

"He had a queue," she offered quietly after a long silence. Queues, long pigtails and shaved foreheads, were worn by all Han Chinese until the fall of the Qing dynasty in the 1920s, when the last Manchu emperor, Puyi, had his own chopped off.

"He would sit on the porch and smoke a long bamboo pipe. I loved the way it smelled. I remember that he was in his 90s and almost blind by then," Granny said, getting a wistful look in her eyes.

The researcher stayed and talked with Granny for another half hour, then gathered up her notes and shook Granny's hand, promising to keep in touch. A year later, a small, bound book arrived: the researcher's published paper. Lily's mother and her sisters passed it around, proud of Granny and the part she had played in its creation.

The memory of Granny now made Lily smile to herself as she started up the rental car. Often when she traveled, Lily felt something that connected her to the places she visited. It wasn't exactly déjà vu. But she felt comfortable and contented.

It would have made Lily's friends laugh to hear her go on like this. They would have told her she was one of those overly dramatic, middle-aged women who longed for a connection to something more exciting than their humdrum, everyday lives. So she kept silent. But her mind traveled back to Ah Chan.

She knew he had become quite successful from sugar and land purchases after the Great Mahele, when King Kamehameha III allowed foreigners to own land in fee simple. By this time, Ah Chan had moved to Hilo from Waimea with his wife, Mahealani, and their young daughter, Kahea.

Her ancestor seemed to Lily to have been a man with modern ideas when it came to the women in his own household. He had made sure that his daughter received a good education at a small private school operated by Lucy Wetmore, the wife of a Christian missionary. He and Mahealani adopted his friend's two children, a boy and a girl, after the friend drowned in Hilo Bay. He even left property and money to his daughter, "free and clear of her husband," in his will. *Now that's enlightenment for his day*, Lily thought.

Mahealani and her daughter were devout Catholics, among the first to be baptized on the islands. But Ah Chan showed no interest in their religion. He may even have distrusted it and considered it a crutch that women and weak men needed. Perhaps he had seen too much in his life.

This made his close friendship with one of the priests at the St. Joseph's Church in Hilo even more surprising. After Mahealani's death, he married again, this time to a much younger woman. He had loved, but he never fooled himself into thinking he was a man who could live alone. He was still Chinese, after all, and needed the support of a robust family.

Shortly after marrying, Ah Chan converted to Catholicism and within months gave the parish some land on which to build a new church. When he died at ninety-five, he was buried in this old Catholic cemetery up the street from the bowling alley and convenience store he had operated for years after giving up sugar.

Ah Chan's fortune by this time was considerable. It supported the next three generations of his family and was something for which everyone was grateful. It meant their large families would be well-housed and educated.

But to Lily, Ah Chan had always been somewhat of a family myth. She wanted concrete evidence he had existed—maybe a marker or headstone would help. She headed up Waianuenue Street, stopped once at the Dairy Queen to make sure the graveyard was still there, then turned into a mostly empty parking lot beside a row of low-income housing.

A little boy of about three had been playing outside near the fence and watched as she got out of her car. His nose was running and his little fingers dirty, but he laughed and smiled at her.

The graveyard looked neglected. A new one had opened across town and more people visited it. Lily opened the small wooden gate barely hanging on its hinges and began looking for family members' names. She found a couple, then more. But still no grave for Ah Chan.

A large tree in the center of the small cemetery provided a leafy shade. Lily wasn't sure what kind of tree it was. She sat near the graves and pulled weeds and long grasses that had grown between them. It was something she remembered Granny Kamanu and Auntie Emma Akau had done every Saturday afternoon when she had been a child on Maui. Cleaning the graves and bringing fresh flowers: the task of widows and women alone, Lily thought. She used to go with them and play between the headstones, trying to peek into crypts that were partially cracked open. It made her sad that these days fewer people took the time to care for them.

After a while, Lily gave up trying to find Ah Chan. She stood and made her way back to the broken cemetery gate and her rental car. But something stopped her. It was nothing specific, just a strong feeling she had given up too soon. She was often impatient. She knew that about herself.

*Okay, Ah Chan, you devil! I'm trying to find you*, she thought quietly. *I may not be religious, but in my heart I believe in magic. Do you want to be found, or not? If you do, you're going to have to pull a trick here because I'm leaving.* Lily laughed at herself for being so silly, but she turned and walked back to the family graves.

The afternoon sun had broken through and the rain had stopped briefly. Behind the graves, Lily noticed the foliage was thickly overgrown from neglect and regular downpours. On pure impulse, she stepped forward, nearly trampling one of the graves, and pushed aside the growth. There, at eye level, were the letters: AH CHAN. They were carved on a pink granite slab almost as tall as Lily. No last name, just Ah Chan.

Tears welled up in Lily's eyes and she shivered slightly, even though there was no breeze. *Magic can happen*, she thought to herself. "You existed," she said quietly. After a few minutes, she turned and headed for the car. She knew she had managed to use up the afternoon, and it was time to get to the airport.

Lily felt a shift. Something changed inside her. It was about belonging to a place, a heritage, a line of people. Without being conscious of it, she had been looking for that kind of knowledge for some time. She understood why Hawaiians revered their ancestors even now. It was not for former glory or wealth, but for the connections they got to places and the land, the *aina*. It tied them, reminding them of who they were, and it made them whole. Knowing of Ah Chan, even if they were separated by all those years, helped Lily feel whole as well. She belonged to something and she wasn't alone. There was a chain that had come before her.

Lily started the engine and made her way down Waianuenue Avenue. She could see a rainbow over the street ahead of her. *So that's where the street got its name*, she thought. *Wai*, fresh water; *anuenue*, rainbow. It made sense. Now everything made sense.

# CLARE

"Mom's had a stroke."

Lily heard the words through the crackling of the long-distance connection. She'd just arrived in Rome, feeling ragged and fuzzy-brained after the transatlantic flight from New York. But her sister's news made her drop to the edge of the bed and take a long, deep breath before she could speak.

"When?" she asked, trying not to look at her husband, David, who had just walked out of the bathroom wearing a quizzical expression. He stood there, his face half covered with shaving cream, looking concerned and a little silly.

Lily's eyes wandered to the rococo carving on the headboard. The faded, old-world lushness of the room, so European, so Roman, made the bright, clear light and colors of Hawaii seem even farther away. She could feel a tiny knot beginning to grow in the pit of her stomach. Her mother had a way of causing this. Even when Lily's news was good, her mother always seemed to have a remark to deflate her, to make the burning begin, make it work its way up into Lily's throat until the tears came.

"It happened last night. I was on the phone with her and all of a sudden she sounded so confused and vague." Jessica was the baby of the family and the closest to their mother. Whenever Lily tried to help Clare, it was Jessica she wanted instead. She wanted Jessica to pick up her papayas from the market each week, insisting she picked the best ones, and it was Jessica who accompanied Clare to the bank once a month to deposit her social security and annuity checks. Just when Lily gave up trying, her mother would call with some cockeyed request that was impossible to grant. *Why can't she just let me win one?* Lily thought.

Lily knew her mother still felt guilty for abandoning Jessica to weeks of rough living on the beach when she had kicked the girl out in a rage. Jessica had been fifteen at the time and never returned home. It had been the children's father, by this time living with his new girlfriend, who had found Jessica, sunburned and hungry at Big Beach in Makena.

Jessica had been born after Lily had left for boarding school in Honolulu. At first, Jessica had just been a squalling, red-faced bundle on the bed in her parents' room, and Lily had paid little attention to her. It wasn't that she hadn't loved Jess; she had hardly known her. *You could barely have considered her a real person at that point*, thought Lily.

By the time Jessica was kicked out of the house, Lily had been married already, living in San Francisco with David and two small children of her own. She'd distanced herself from her life in Hawaii, chalked it up as having way too much drama for her tastes. Their brother Hank was overseas in Vietnam and out of touch. Her father had moved in with the new girlfriend, which had ramped her mother up into a familiar frenzy followed by a series of tantrums. *Enough*, thought Lily. *Enough.*

Clare had left Maui shortly after Jessica was found. First she had sent cards from Barcelona, then from the Mexican art colony in San Miguel de Allende. Lily suspected her mother, with her smoky darkness, had liked passing for a local in Latin countries. Her mother had finally settled on a dude ranch resort in the Santa Inez Valley near Santa Barbara, where she arranged trail rides and bingo games for guests.

It had taken Clare twenty years to return to Maui. And when she did, she behaved as if no time had passed and she could simply pick up being everyone's mother again. *I thought it was the kids who were supposed to be wayward*, thought Lily.

Back in the hotel room, she snapped to, suddenly realizing she was no longer listening to Jessica.

"I'll get a flight and come right back." It was the last thing Lily wanted to do. She'd looked forward to this trip for ages, but her mother had had a stroke, for Christ's sake. Clare had always had a way of throwing a bomb in things. Lily stopped herself.

"Oh, don't," said Jessica. "She's in the hospital, she's fine, and we're all here. She'll get better. Have a good time, Lily. I just wanted you to know so you wouldn't be surprised or mad at me for not telling you when you return."

"Okay, Jessica. But be sure to let me know how she's doing. I'm going to call you, you hear? I'll call."

Lily hung up the phone. *Damn*. What she needed was sleep. When she woke, she'd call Jessica back and tell her she'd changed her mind and was coming home. But Jessica didn't seem concerned. She looked over at David, who lay curled up on the other side of the bed. He'd obviously not overhead the conversation because he was already sound asleep, snoring contentedly. Lily climbed in beside him, still wearing the clothes she'd worn across the U.S. and the Atlantic. "I guess we're not going out for lunch," she said softly. Soon, she too fell into a deep sleep.

IT WAS LATE AFTERNOON WHEN LILY opened her eyes. The sun cast slanted ribbons of light across the bed. For a moment, she wasn't sure where she was. She looked at the clock beside the bed. She'd slept all day. She turned to see if David was beside her, but the bed was empty. There was a note on the nightstand saying he'd gone to explore the neighborhood for a restaurant where they could have dinner.

Lily rolled over and stared at the ceiling for a few minutes before deciding to call Jessica back. She wondered what the time difference was, suspecting it would be the middle of the night in Hawaii. But she decided she didn't care. Now that she was less tired, she needed more information. She reached for the phone, then dialed the long-distance line, the country code, then her sister's number.

"Yeah?" Jessica sounded sleepy and grumpy.

"It's me again. Now tell me exactly how Mom is."

"Oh, Lily, for chrissake. Do you know what time it is here?"

"Sorry, but I need to know. Should I come back?"

"No, no. I told you already. She's going to be fine. Come home when your trip is over."

"Okay, sorry I woke you, go back to sleep." Lily hung up.

LILY AND DAVID SPENT THE NEXT few days visiting all their favorite Rome spots, including the little café in Trastevere. She tried not to think of her mother lying in Maui Memorial Hospital. Jessica had assured her Clare would be all right. There was no need for Lily to come back. Things were handled. *They had better be, Jess,* she thought.

She and David took a taxi over the Ponte Sisto, the bridge over the Tiber that led into the old working-class neighborhood they had haunted as students. They loved the big piazza, with the twelfth-century Basilica de Santa Maria Maggiore at one end, a fountain at the center, and cafés where you could people watch for hours for the price of a cappuccino. The crowded little shops on the narrow, cobbled side streets burst with brightly painted ceramics, aromatic olive oils, and sticky candies stuffed with pistachios. Colorful begonias and bougainvillea adorned balconies and spilled from planters obscuring the faded walls, the paint scrubbed by time. It seemed so long ago that they had been here, but still the smell of sauces filled with garlic and the immediate honks of Vespas remained, tugging at their hearts and making them wish they were young again and had the gift of foresight.

Had she and David ever had so much to talk about that they had stayed up until after midnight? She could hardly remember. David was a good husband and father. He was steady, dependable, and he loved her, she knew that. But the excitement had gone out of their relationship, and she found herself fantasizing about being alone again with the possibility for new adventures. It wasn't that anything was wrong with their marriage; it just seemed to have gone a bit flat. The thought came to her that she needed to do something about it. Maybe this trip would jumpstart their marriage and inject some of those old feelings. Too much comfort in a relationship sure wasn't what it was cracked up to be. Maybe growing up with Clare and Buddy as parents had addicted Lily to chaos so that uproar was what she sought out, even craved.

On the third day in Rome, after visits to their familiar, crowded neighborhood near the Vatican and the hangout near the Piazza Navona, where they used to go with their friends every Friday night, they packed their bags and picked up a rental car. It took them an hour to find their way through traffic and out of the city. Lily attempted to read the map and follow the directions given at the rental office, but David was getting more and more irritated at their wrong turns. She wondered why they hadn't sprung for the GPS. Rome was impossible to navigate. This happened every time they were on a trip. By the time they hit the highway, David was in a fury, swearing at Italian drivers and driving way too fast. It made Lily want to swat him, but instead she settled into an exasperated silence.

Finally, they were nicely humming along on the highway to Spoleto. Lily started thinking about her mother again. It seemed impossible not to. Clare was one complicated woman. Attractive still, even at eighty-six, and barely five feet tall, she'd married Buddy just after her eighteenth birthday. He was, by then, nearly thirty years old. Buddy loved telling Lily, Hank and Jessica about the day they'd met. Clare and two other Hawaiian girls sat in the middle of the road in front of her house in Wailuku playing a game of jacks, not having much luck with the uneven surface of the road. He'd come around the corner in his car, slammed on the brakes not a moment too soon, and landed in her grandmother's hibiscus hedge. In spite of the racket he caused, Clare barely looked up. When she did, a smile broke across her face that was both challenging and triumphant. She stared straight at him with the biggest brown eyes he'd ever seen.

"Take it easy, Buster," she said, in a gravelly voice that made her seem older and warier than she actually was, before returning to her impossible game of jacks. That was it, just, "Take it easy, Buster." *That's a lotta damn nerve,* Buddy thought. For a moment, he considered scolding these sassy Hawaiian kids. But he thought better of it, shrugged, put the car in reverse, carefully maneuvering around the girls, and drove off still thinking of those brown eyes. Clare had nerve in spades, but Buddy had no way of knowing that then. She was a pretty local girl. The kind he found hard to resist.

AFTER A NIGHT IN SPOLETO, LILY and David drove to the hill town of Assisi, parked outside the old city, and dragged their suitcases over the bumpy cobblestones to the inn they'd selected specifically for its views of the green valley below and its well-reviewed restaurant. Lily had never been to Assisi, and David was eager to show her the muraled walls by Giotto on the Basilica Papale di San Francesco. David seemed to have rediscovered his Catholic faith in the last year, going to mass regularly again and making sure he supported the local parish. These things now meant so much to him. Lily's faith in religion, on the other hand, seemed to have grown less as the years passed. Still, she didn't interfere and instead let him have whatever comfort he needed. *Life is hard enough,* she thought.

That night, she lay awake and stared at the stars painted on the stucco ceiling of their hotel room. The room was dimly lit from the café next door, and the conversations, mostly in Italian, drifted upstairs. She thought about her mother again. She had called every day, but there was no change in the news. "She's fine. Stop worrying, Have a good time," was all Jessica would say.

Lily began to wonder how she really felt about her mother. She had loved her desperately as a child. In those days, Clare always had been home with them, taken them to the beach and to picnics in Rainbow Park on the winding road to Makawao Town. She had taken them to the doctor, the dentist, and swimming lessons after school. Lily had never noticed that her mother hadn't ever cooked a meal or ironed a shirt. That had been done, instead, by the steady parade of young maids who had been delivered from the local detention home. Several of the young maids had been friends of Clare's more than just wards of the court. One young Portuguese girl named Aggie actually had become a lifelong friend of Clare's. There was, after all, less than a decade in age between them. Perhaps they had shared an island of localness in the mostly haole plantation neighborhood.

ALL FAMILIES HAVE THEIR STORIES. THEY'RE told and retold over dinner tables and in living rooms when relatives visit. Lily, Hank, and Jessica had heard the story of how Clare had hauled off and decked a rival politician of Buddy's so many times they had lost count. Yet it still thrilled them enough to listen to the retelling, a familiar, comforting refrain that explained their own feisty natures.

Buddy Donahue had run for various state and county positions over the years as a moderate Republican (moderate meaning he wasn't completely bought and paid for by his plantation bosses). But on this night, Clare had created a scene at the County Fairgrounds that caused a stir among the onlookers and a delight that lasted for years with her offspring.

To be fair, the 1950s were a volatile time in Hawaii. Japanese-American veterans were returning to take advantage of the G.I. Bill, and labor movements among the working plantation population caught fire. There had been unrest in the past, but this time the dissent had some teeth with the help of West Coast labor leaders like Harry Bridges and Jack Hall.

Buddy Donahue was a handsome, charming creature considered by many of his contemporary plantation colleagues to be charismatic, but not quite one of them. He had no interest in their after-work cocktails and preferred hanging out with his local friends fishing and playing *hanafuda* cards. Word got around that he raised high-quality fighting chickens for the camp chicken fights, and it was known that Filipino men regularly showed up at the Donahue house with wads of cash rolled up with rubber bands in order to purchase his remarkable birds. Even worse, he attended a regular card game in the Japanese camp with a childhood friend. Then, of course, there was his part-Hawaiian wife.

But Buddy was made for politics, with his dazzling smile, his mouth wide with gleaming white teeth, his streaked blond surfer hair, and his decided gift of gab regardless of the racial mix of his audience. He had already been elected to the Territorial Constitutional Convention and, within a year, to the Territorial House of Representatives, but the mood in Hawaii had changed. This election was going to be no piece of cake.

Johnny Tavares, a particularly crude street fighter of a man, was running against Buddy. His attacks, filled with the usual lies and innuendos, were particularly nasty for the time and uncharacteristic for rural elections filled with flower leis, music, and campaigning on the backs of flatbed trucks festooned with palm fronds. That night, Tavares was no different. Only Clare had had enough of his insinuations about Buddy, and on that Friday night at the Kahului Fairgrounds, she let him have it.

Tavares stood on stage at the microphone, his aloha shirt untucked, spewing his usual hate speech to a rapt crowd already primed to listen. "You want to go on electing haole assholes like Donahue, you go right ahead," he was saying. "I'm one local, I know you folks, and I gone fight for you. Dump that haole trash. Vote for me and I will—aaghhhhhhhh!"

Tavares had stopped speaking, and banging and thudding sounds were heard over the loudspeakers. The stunned crowd and those on the perimeters chewing on candy apples and downing cones of chow fun turned to see what was going on. The microphone toppled to the floor, and a stunned Tavares staggered backward toward the palms and pots of red ginger behind him. He wasn't down, but he was clearly stunned as a look of confusion and disbelief, followed by red rage, filled his face.

Standing in front of him and a little off to the side was Clare, in her usual black pedal pushers paired with a pristine turquoise blouse, all five feet of her—erect, angry. Her fists were still clenched, perfectly red-lacquered nails biting into the palms of her hands.

Tavares's face contorted with hate as he regained his stance and lunged back at her in front of what now was a crowd of about a hundred people, his fists cocked. It was evident that if it hadn't been for his own handlers, he would have slugged Clare with such force she would have flown off the stage in front of the crowd.

The crowd stood shocked as Tavares was escorted off the stage, and Buddy collected Clare, tucking her into the back of their green Pontiac for the ride back to Paia. They stopped in Lower Paia, where Buddy ran into Harada Market for a bottle of Jack Daniels and some aspirin before they headed up to their house above the mill.

In November, Buddy was elected to a second term.

WHEN CLARE GOT A JOB AS the librarian in Paia's small public library, Lily, Hank and Jessica spent all their after-school time there reading as their mother stamped books at checkout and charmed the old men who came in each week for a new book. They explored prehistoric worlds filled with swamps; exotic, predatory plants; and menacing animals. They flew in their minds to planets at the far reaches of the universe. It was Clare's doing—Clare with her hunger for life, her feisty spirit and need to know about everything beyond the island she had never left except to spend summers with her cousins in Hilo and make occasional shopping trips to Honolulu.

Clare had grown up in a time when being Hawaiian was not the proud heritage it is today. In spite of that, she always was aware of who she was and was proud. As a result, Lily, Hank, and Jessica were also proud to be part Hawaiian.

Clare's father worked as an accountant in Wailuku and her mother taught at the local elementary school. She was the youngest of four girls, all of whom were headed for secretarial jobs and marriage. There was never any thought of college, even though Clare graduated at the top of her class in high school.

It wasn't until she was much older, after her marriage and the children—after the so-called Hawaiian renaissance, the reawakening, took place in the 1970s—when Clare decided to embrace her ethnicity more openly. Before that she had held the unspoken belief that marrying a haole and joining plantation society was what every reasonable woman wanted. There'd be no working-class men for her. She had no intention of slaving and scrimping with a local man. At least, she had started out thinking that way. But that was another time and things were changing.

Lily's grandmother had never let Clare and her sisters learn to swim. Perhaps because they'd spend all their time at the beach and get too brown. "You want to look like a *popolo*?" Popolos were tiny blue-black berries used in local medicine, but everyone understood the term meant someone of African heritage. Not a good thing, even though few on the island had ever laid eyes on an African, or negro, as everyone called them back then. So in 1978, Clare signed up for swimming lessons at the community pool in Wailuku. What did she care how dark she got? She was Hawaiian. She wanted to swim.

Shortly after Clare returned to Maui, she hit a dog one night while driving home to her new house in Waihee. Rather than stop on the remote and dark road, she kept going until she pulled into her driveway and garage. The little wooden house was near the ocean but obscured from it by a thick, dark tangle of hau trees. Terrified, she stepped out of the car and checked the sandy ground in front of her car. The dog must have been impaled on the grill as she drove, because it now lay on the ground in front of the car. Clare's stomach turned. All those stories she'd heard when she was a child came rushing back. *Behave yourself or someone will "kahuna you." Watch out—if someone hates you or is jealous, they'll put a spell on you.* Was this a sign, an omen? Who could be jealous of her? But she was too tired to be properly fearful, decided to deal with the dead dog in morning, and went to bed, shaken. In the morning, there was no sign of the dog.

That settled it. If there had been a real dog, it would still be lying there, or at least nearby. No dog surely meant evil was directed at her. Someone was out to get her; she knew it in her bones. She'd ask around. She needed a lot of help to throw off the curse.

The dog episode sent Clare straight to a *kahuna*, or shaman, not the Catholic priest in her Waihee parish. The Belgian with the barely intelligible sermons couldn't fix this. She needed bigger magic. The kahuna would pray and tell her who wished her ill. It must be Buddy's new girlfriend. "That kanaka bitch. I know how they are. But I have a kahuna too. She can't do this to me!" That led to several visits to the traditional healer. Lily and Jessica, aware of their mother's solution to her fears, wondered if Clare ever confessed to her priest that she had slipped into witchcraft without consulting the church. But they doubted Clare saw any conflict. The church was for going to heaven, but kahunas had their place for this kind of bad business.

About six months later, Clare began taking Hawaiian language classes at night at the local high school. After two months she gave up. "It was too hard," she told Lily. "I'm too old to learn a language."

Now that Clare was settled at home again after the dog incident and sure the curse had no power over her, she seemed a little at odds with Lily. "Who do you think you are, Martha Stewart?" she'd say when Lily wanted a pretty Easter brunch with linen and flowers.

"Nah, paper plates good enough. Your beach place is nice." Lily was now in her forties and successful enough in real estate to buy a small house on the beach outside Paia with a large lawn and palm trees fronting the sand. It was a score and she and David knew it. They'd slipped easily into the local social scene, which by this time had dropped plantation ways and was looking ahead to a different kind of prosperous time.

"Let's invite Auntie Iwalani and Uncle and all the kids. Uncle can bring the *pulehu* meat and grill outside. It'll be good fun. Nobody wants all that fancy stuff, Lily," her mother said.

It seemed to Lily that her mother had pointed her in one direction, only to switch midstream. It left Lily feeling as if she herself were rigid and fussy. She liked the flower pots filled with hydrangeas and the little savory biscuits filled with Kentucky ham and strong mustard. She liked real eggs dyed pastel and decorated by hand. Leave it to Auntie Iwalani or Jessica and you'd get those bilious plastic eggs from Longs Drugs filled with cheap chocolates. Their kids were too old for egg hunts now anyway. They'd just as soon be on the beach out of sight sharing a toke of weed and checking out the waves. Jeez, life with Clare back in it was no picnic.

THE CALL FROM JESSICA CAME THE day Lily and David arrived at JFK for their return trip home. They made their way through customs and took the airport shuttle to the Marriott for the night before heading up to Massachusetts for David's college reunion. They'd piggybacked the trip to Italy with his reunion, thinking it made sense and would save them some money.

"Oh, thank God I got you!" It was Jessica, suddenly relieved. "Oh, Lily, Lily. I'm so sorry. Please don't be mad at me. Everything was going along so well. It just all happened so quickly." Lily went cold. "We were all singing to her—Auntie Emma, Auntie Iwalani, Kalei, Pono, Hank, Crazy Anna brought the Hawaiian kahuna, the whole bit. She just closed her eyes and died, Lily. No one expected it; we were all singing to her. She closed those big beautiful *makas* and she was gone."

Lily sat still staring at the digital clock on the nightstand. She hated those clocks. So often they were set by previous guests and went off at the worst times. She'd once thrown one across the room in exasperation.

"It's okay, Jess," she said quietly.

"I've got Kalei booking you on a flight home right now, Lily. Let David go to his reunion, I know you'd want to be here. I'm so, so sorry."

"Thanks, Jess."

*Breathe*, Lily thought, *breathe*. The room was silent and still, and down the hall she heard the elevator open and guests step out laughing.

"It's weird, Lily. That kahuna was holding her hand and speaking to her in Hawaiian, and I swear she understood every word. Really, Lily. I didn't understand a thing, but Mom seemed to. Isn't that strange?

Lily nodded, "Yeah, Jess. Strange."

# BALI

In the months following her mother's death, Lily realized she felt on edge and ever so slightly angry. She thought she hid it well as she went about her day, picking up the cleaning, doing the grocery shopping, and making dinners at night. But it must have been more obvious than she thought, because when an offer came to go to Bali for a week with some old college girlfriends, she got no resistance from David. Instead, he urged her to go, telling her it was just what she needed.

That was the way David always was with her. He accommodated her mercurial moods that seemed to rise from nowhere, surprising them both with their intensity. She was like her mother, she knew that, and it irritated her. She'd always tried to be calm and reasonable during her life with David, never wanting to shout ultimatums or throw temper tantrums. But David knew better. He knew she often smoldered. The fact that he loved her in spite of her quirkiness filled her with both warmth and irritation over the fact that he didn't try to stop her when she slipped into those dark places. He was always so damn understanding.

She felt an urge to run away whenever she was confronted with difficult life changes. This had become a pattern since her late teens. Each time things got tough, she ran.

She and David had two grown children, but were now caught up in their own lives. At forty-five, she was happy it was just the two of them again. David didn't seem to mind either. He was content with his work as an architect, and when she was away on one of her trips, he gardened and played golf with his friends.

"Where are you off to now, toots?" he'd ask, pulling her down onto his lap, snuggling his face into her hair.

She'd fake a pout, but with David she could never keep it up for long. Still, it was good she was going to get away. It would give her time to try to put her feelings about Clare's passing in some sort of perspective.

She was like Clare in so many ways. She too had a passion for books and people. Her moods could slip from high to low with such dizzying speed one had to be on one's toes to keep up with her. Lily had tried to hide the mercurial moods by always doing the right thing and steering away from situations she or others would consider dangerous. She often wondered what kind of price she had paid in doing this. Had not wanting to be like Clare kept her from fully living her life? *Maybe*, she thought.

ON MONDAY, SHE BOOKED HER FLIGHT to Bali and began hunting for her passport, which she finally found tossed into a basket in her closet filled with empty boxes that had once held costume jewelry and a bottle of stray buttons. Lily's college friends arranged to meet her in the cool mountain village of Ubud, about an hour from the airport in Denpasar. But with flights leaving only twice a week from Honolulu, she was going to have to spend a couple of days on her own before her friends arrived from a side jaunt they had planned to Java.

The next Friday, she packed only a carry-on, and David drove her to the airport.

"Don't bother to pack much. There are so many cool things to buy when you get there," said her old college roommate, Jody. She worked for a Los Angeles interior design firm and seemed to spend half her time in Bali creating coffee tables that looked like rough slabs of wood on spiral steel bases and platform beds any minimalist would swoon over.

As Lily's flight approached the airport at Denpasar, she could see volcanoes rising from the land everywhere. They weren't the smoothly sloped volcanoes she saw in Hawaii; these rose up dramatically from the land. On top of each volcanic mound was a small crater. The effect was unreal, like a simplistic cartoon drawn by a grade school child. You expected to find King Kong living in the jungles below.

The airport had grown much busier since the first time she had visited Bali in the early 1990s. There were long lines of people now, waiting to get through customs, and outside the airport taxi drivers yelled and gestured to her, wanting to take her to her hotel or perhaps serve as private guides for the remainder of her visit.

Lily listened for her name and within minutes found Putu, the driver she had hired to take her from the sweltering lowlands to cooler Ubud. The town had once been a village of Balinese artists and craftsmen. She had heard from Jody that the Balinese remained as gentle and polite as they had always been. Only now, interspersed on the streets and in the shops, were many Australians, French, and Italians. Some had come for vacations, gone home, quit their jobs, and came back to live. Others ran businesses that made stylish clothing and housewares for upscale shoppers.

She checked into the Barong Resort in town near the Monkey Forest and spent most of the next day sweltering in the white-hot heat, ducking in and out of shops lining Monkey Forest Road. The wares she noticed were much more European-looking and sophisticated than those she'd seen on her first trip. Gone were the gaudily carved images painted bright colors and trimmed in gold. They had been replaced with high-style terrazzo sinks and bath tubs, sheer-white cotton dresses, and crisp linen duvets and bedding.

Lily purchased an exquisitely painted egg. It was a useless object, but it reminded her of the sort of thing that had filled tables in her mother's condo. It was a nod to her mother's passing, she thought.

Tired and feeling jet-lagged, she walked back to the hotel, where she lay on her bed under the mosquito netting she hoped would keep all the crawly critters at bay and watched the fan overhead turn slowly. She could have turned on the air conditioning, but the fan-cooled air made her feel like she was in one of those old black and white movies of her childhood.

After a short nap, she called a Balinese friend of Jody's named Wayan. Jody had insisted she take his phone number, though Lily had resisted. But the thought of spending the evening alone in her hotel room with room service and a book seemed like a waste in this exotic place. Maybe he could meet her for a quick drink? She wasn't sure Balinese men drank, but he could order a Coke or some tea, she thought.

Every other man in Bali seemed to be called Wayan. She remembered that from before. Balinese men each had a handful, four or so names, which indicated the order of their birth. They were named either Wayan, Made, Nyoman, or Ketut. If there was a fifth child, they started all over again, this time with Wayan Balik (or "Wayan Again"). It had something to do with the Hindu caste system, and she was sure there were variations.

Lily picked up the phone beside her bed and punched in the number. A man with a deep voice answered after the first ring and it surprised her. For a second, she wasn't sure she'd done the right thing, but she resisted the impulse to hang up.

"Hello, Wayan?" Did she sound anxious?

"Yes." The voice on the other end of the line hesitated for a second.

"This is Lily Cunningham. I'm the school friend Jody Barnes emailed you about." She tried to sound upbeat and casually friendly.

"Ah, Lily. Yes, I've been waiting for your call," he answered in perfect, barely accented English. "I'm sorry to hear about your mother's recent death. Jody told me all about you. I understand you've been to Bali before."

"Yes, but Jody swears you would know everything about this place. It's been so long, and I really never got beyond the beaches at Legian on my last visit." She was suddenly shy and nervous. This was a complete stranger, a man in a foreign land, even if he was a friend of a friend.

"Have you been to the temple to see the *Ramayana* yet?" he asked. "I have to go there tonight, and I think you might enjoy it. Tourists often come as well as the local people."

"I'd love to," said Lily. She never had been comfortable meeting a man in a bar, but this was different.

"I'll pick you up at six. Where are you staying?"

"At the Barong near the Monkey Forest."

"Okay. I'll be at your hotel at six. Look for a green Land Rover," he said.

Lily hung up the phone and wondered how she was going to tell David about this night. Would it upset him? Would he feel threatened? *Oh, hell*, she thought. *Just tell the truth.* It was always best.

But Lily couldn't ignore the thrill of hearing the voice of an unfamiliar man on the other end of the line. It felt a little dangerous. A little like being Clare, she realized.

She guessed he was about the same age as she, maybe a little younger. She wished she could remember whether Jody had said if he was married or not. What did that matter, she thought, throwing herself on the bamboo bed and pulling the mosquito net around her.

Lily watched the overhead fan circle slowly again. This situation wouldn't have bothered Clare in the least. She could see her mother, her dark curls askew and large black eyes. For Clare it would have been a thrill. Another adventure to add to her long string of adventures. Lily felt more alive than she had in months.

She dozed off and awoke feeling groggy and lethargic. She headed for the shower in a bathroom made of sleek wood and stone.

Descending into the deep, sunken bathtub, she turned on the overhead shower and stared out the window at the surrounding garden, letting the water wash away the sleep. *The Balinese really know how to do baths*, she thought.

Refreshed, she threw on a light linen shift and at the last minute grabbed a cotton sweater for modesty's sake. After all, this was a temple, and from what she had observed the Balinese were modest people.

Lily caught a glimpse of herself in the mirror as she headed for the door. *Hmm, not too bad for an old broad*, she thought as she flipped on an inside light so she wouldn't have to enter a dark room when she returned that night.

Wayan was right on time. He jumped out of the Land Rover and headed directly for her.

"Lily! You must be Lily," he smiled a toothy, almost tour-guide-like grin, putting his hand out toward her.

She climbed into the car, but not before she noticed a small offering basket made of coconut fronds and filled with marigolds and plumeria on the dashboard of the car.

Wayan seemed a little out of breath. "I think I forgot to mention on the phone that I'm actually in the re-enactment tonight. I hope you don't mind. I've spent so much time away from Bali and my culture, I thought it was time I got back into it."

He shifted the Land Rover and backed onto Monkey Forest Road, barely avoiding a young hippie couple dressed in a lot of sheer gauze.

Lily tried to check him out without his knowing. She was sure he was doing the same thing with her but she brushed the thought out of her mind.

His hair was very black with a slightly receding hairline above smooth, brown, unlined skin. He was only a little taller than Lily, and his build was strong and muscular. *Almost stocky*, she thought to herself.

"The *Ramayana* is one of the oldest of our Hindu epic stories," he said. "It shows us the righteous path and our duties in this life. It's a little long, but I think you'll find it beautiful and exciting."

"I'm sure I will. Human values are much the same in all cultures, don't you think?"

Wayan looked over at her and then back at the road. But he didn't answer.

Lily gazed out the window at the galleries and shops she'd visited earlier in the day. They would be closed by the time she returned. She hadn't had anything to eat since lunch at the Dirty Duck and wondered if Wayan would suggest they get something to eat after the performance. Maybe at Made's, where Jody's expat friends hung out. On second thought, she didn't suppose that was his scene.

The Land Rover pulled up in front of the temple. They were at the edge of town, and a crowd of mostly men and some tourists gathered outside.

"Stay right here. I'll pick up your ticket." Wayan leaped out of the car and up the stairs to the ticket kiosk. On the way up, he shouted greetings at several men standing nearby. It reminded Lily of the way local guys in Hawaii behaved when they were out with haole girls and bumped into their old buddies.

He was back shortly with the tickets and told her to go inside and get herself a good seat. Lily jumped out and made her way up the stairs through the intricately carved gates into the interior courtyard of the temple.

Chairs were set up on three sides of an open space facing an edifice of stone with vines growing randomly over much of it. She assumed the drama would be played out in the open area and took a seat in the front row.

As soon as it was dark the drama began. Male and female actors danced and moved to the clanging of the gamelan. They were dressed in elaborate costumes of gold and colored cloth and all wore masks. Lily was glad she'd done a little reading ahead of time so that she could follow the action. She realized she had forgotten to ask Wayan what role he played, so she didn't know to whom she should pay particular attention. She could discuss it with him later.

In the drama, the god Rama and his consort, Sita, embark on a tale of betrayal, flight, and survival. Sita, the god's faithful wife, steps out of a magic circle in which she is protected and gets herself kidnapped. But she is rescued by the monkey king, Hanuman.

Lily noticed the actor playing Hanuman was muscular and stocky. She wondered if it was Wayan behind the mask.

After the play, a large bonfire was lit in the center of the courtyard. The evening ended with a *kecak*, or fire dance. The dance was based on an old ritual but had been shortened over the years, making it easier on the audience. As the dancers moved around the fire to the rhythms, the drums got louder and faster, and several dancers seemed to go into trances, kicking fiery bits of debris toward the audience, making them shriek. The tourists seemed the most bothered by the flying fireballs.

All Lily could feel was the mosquitoes dive-bombing around her ankles and the back of her neck. Thank goodness she'd applied repellant and brought a sweater.

As one dancer broke from the group in a frenzy, she wondered whether they required fire safety permits in Bali. Probably not. Nothing else seemed to be regulated.

After the performance, Lily made her way through the crowd to the front of the temple. She waited on the top step for a few minutes, looking for Wayan and the Land Rover. The night seemed very dark now, and there were only a few random streetlights. The light was so dim, she hoped Wayan would see her. But he did.

She climbed back into the Land Rover and they started down, of all places, she thought, Hanuman Street.

"That was wonderful," she said to Wayan.

"I'm glad you enjoyed it." He looked over at her and smiled. He seemed exhausted as they bumped down Hanuman a few blocks and turned onto a small, even darker side street. Within a minute they were at another intersection.

The town was buttoned up tightly, and every now and then Lily caught a glimpse of stray dogs crossing the road. A couple of dogs sported coats dyed red, green, or blue. Some sort of food coloring, she decided. This was a funny culture.

Wayan stopped the car abruptly at the corner. "You can get out right here. Your hotel is just down the street that way. I'm glad you enjoyed the performance." He smiled, but he was clearly not going to take her to her front door.

Lily was stunned. It wasn't that she expected him to entertain her all night, but, truthfully, she'd wanted a little more. Some conversation, maybe?

She saw a group of men across the street by the light of an open café. They were laughing and she got a whiff of clove cigarettes, or was it something else?

No. This didn't feel good. Was she really going to have her find her own way? Had he no manners?

But instead of demanding he take her to her front door, Lily climbed out onto the street.

"Oh, of course. I enjoyed the evening so much."

She wasn't sure he heard her as the door slammed. She thought she saw Wayan wave as the Land Rover headed back in the other direction.

Lily stood in the dark for a minute. It seemed longer. Then she started walking in the direction he'd indicated. It was dark. Very dark. She was afraid of falling into those gaping holes in the street she'd noticed during the day. The sidewalks buckled in places, and there were dangerous holes in them, too. She decided to stick to walking in the street.

She heard the men in the café burst into loud laughter, and it forced her to walk faster. *Damn!* What would her mother have done? Lily knew she wouldn't have gotten out of the car. Clare had been a diva. She would have demanded to be taken to the front of her hotel.

Lily's heart was pounding now. She hated the dark, hated this strange place. She wanted to be home with David. What had she been thinking? She chose safe. She liked safe.

She was almost running now. For a moment she wasn't sure her hotel was even on this street. Nothing looked familiar. The stores were locked up tight and the only light now was in the distance. She began running.

Then, without warning, a man stepped toward her from the shadows on the side of the road.

"May I help you, ma'am?" he said in English.

Lily jumped back and let out an involuntary yelp. Then she recognized the nice young front desk clerk from the Barong.

"Where are you going, Mrs. Cunningham?"

"Oh, hello." Lily was embarrassed at being caught frightened. "I'm afraid I lost my way. But I'm all right now, thank you."

"Are you sure?" The clerk had the sweetest, most reassuring face. "I'm off duty, but I'm happy to see you to your *bale*."

"Oh, no, no. I'm fine."

Lily realized she was in front of the Barong. She made her way through the landscaped foliage to her quarters and opened the heavy wooden door, letting herself into her private courtyard. Once in her room, she locked the door and threw herself on the bed. Her heart still pounded, but she was calming down now.

*I'm not Clare*, she thought to herself. *I'm me. I'm different. I like my life with David, my so-called boring life with David. I like knowing what tomorrow will bring and that I can count on certain things.*

Lily was surprised at how happy this made her feel. She'd always felt a little guilty over not having Clare's sense of adventure and endless ability to live life on the edge. But she realized she didn't feel that anymore.

She climbed into her nightgown and read a few paragraphs in her book. Jody would be here in a few days. Maybe she'd spend tomorrow at the hotel spa, she thought. Within a few minutes she was sleeping soundly.

# ACKNOWLEDGMENTS

HAWAII'S PLANTATION STORY HAS BEEN WELL-DOCUMENTED in historical works and fiction-based-on-truth novels of hardship and struggle. The stories in this book reflect the lives, in the 1940s and 1950s, of families who were more privileged than field workers – many of them doctors, accountants, shop owners and middle managers. They too are deeply rooted in the fabric of the islands. The plantations and their camps are totally gone today, replaced by development and tourism. This book adds their stories to the cultural map of the islands.

I would like to thank my family on Maui - Ken "Woozer" Goring and Stewart Roley and my step-daughters, Joelle Fraser and Marion Philpotts-Miller for their support in writing these stories. My sisters, Dani Ho and Robbie St. Sure and brother, Charlie were wonderful helping me "remember."

Without my writer's group including Rita Ariyoshi, Thelma Chang, Carol Catanzariti, Jodi Belknap and the late Mary Bell I would never have done the work. Supportive friends Carol Hartley Chapman, Betty Fullard-Leo, Mary Dikon, Susie Fitzgerald and Gretchen Duplanty were indispensible.

Thank you to Sarah Katreen Hoggatt of Lucky Bat Books for the hand-holding and Nuno Moreira for the cover design.

Most of all, thanks to my husband, Doug Philpotts, for his support and belief in me and Hawaii's stories.

# AUTHOR BIOGRAPHY

Kaui Philpotts is a writer living in Honolulu. Her previous non-fiction works include *Hawaii: A Sense of Place* with Mary Philpotts McGrath, *Party Hawaii, Floral Traditions: The Honolulu Academy of Arts* and *Hawaiian Country Tables.* This is her first attempt at fiction.

CPSIA information can be obtained
at www.ICGtesting.com
Printed in the USA
JSHW031350050420
5003JS00001B/156

9 781732 786707